The Boy Who Could Bee

Rowan Gordon

Illustrations by Kim Lynch

Jamestowne Bookworks, Williamsburg, Virginia

This is a work of fiction. Any resemblance to real-life people or places is unintentional, except to honour the late Brother Adam of Buckfast Abbey.

Jamestowne Bookworks, Williamsburg, Virginia
©2022 by Jamestowne Bookworks
All Rights Reserved. Published 2022
ISBN 979-8-9852323-1-8 (ebook)
ISBN 979-8-9852323-2-5 (paperback)
ISBN 979-8-9852323-3-2 (hardcover)
The British Library holds a CIP catalogue record
Library of Congress Control Number 2021924315

Summary
A boy and girl and an old monk—Juvenile fiction
Beekeeping in an English monastery—Fiction
Peace and war in a hive of prize honeybees—Fiction
Children unveil a mystery left by medieval monks—Fiction

Jamestowne Bookworks LLC
Shire House, 107 Paddock Lane
Williamsburg, Virginia 23188

Front cover art by Elizabeth Ogle

For Pippa and Sam

Peace to all bees and their carers under the *Sunne*

Contents

Talking of Bees	vii
A Lexicon for Bee	ix
Chapter 1. Sting in the Tail	1
Chapter 2. A New Mutant	17
Chapter 3. Cruel and Unusual Punishment	29
Chapter 4. Hail the Sunne	47
Chapter 5. Has Joe got Talent?	67
Chapter 6. Path to the Vampire Vault	85
Chapter 7. Test of Nerves	93
Chapter 8. The Troubles	101
Chapter 9. The Oldburgh Mystery	117
Chapter 10. Sage Lessons	135
Chapter 11. A Dare in the Dark	151
Chapter 12. Maiden Flight	163

Chapter 13. Pity the Critters	173
Chapter 14. Second Birth	183
Chapter 15. Surprise in the Spinney	203
Chapter 16. The Wanderer Returns	213
Chapter 17. Chasing a Beeline	225
Chapter 18. The Phoney Peace	243
Chapter 19. A Blessed Bone	259
Chapter 20. Aftermath	275
Saying Thanks	287

Talking of Bees

Honeybees can't talk like us, but they need a language. Hive workers share instructions for building a home. Field bees receive directions to gather food. And communication keeps the family at peace. Did I write 'peace'? Ahem. More about that later.

Nothing is better than talking to give and receive information. Sometimes, however, we use sign language to express feelings, needs and wants. I remember the exuberant hi-fives we gave our team on winning at sports days. A lady at my school kept us safe from traffic by holding up her arms at the crossing. And don't forget the smells. They carry messages to turn heads, like the aroma of cinnamon apple pie.

Bees are chatterboxes, but they use sounds, smells, signs and even dance instead of words. These are codes for a language called Bee, translated into Old English nouns in this book. A hive couldn't be an intelligent family of insects without it. If you have watched bees closely, you know they aren't as dim-witted as people think. They depend on instincts, of course, but also make careful choices and are a lot brighter than the average robot, in my view. I doubt they have any self-awareness, but I dare say that each has a 'personality' marking them as different from the next bee. Some might even call it a soul.

The monk Brother Adam lived close to bees throughout his long life and never lost a sense of wonder. He talked and listened to them buzzing around his hives, but neither understood the other. He cared for them, never taking too much honey and got irritated when people swatted them for getting too close. The real-life monk died in his monastery in 1996, only two years short of a centenarian. His name and fame are resurrected here in a fictional character.

Forty years ago, the village boy Joe and his older cousin Emily from London spent the summer holidays helping the monk in a Devonshire bee-yard. They didn't realise that the grumpy beekeeper and his stinging insects were joint guardians of an ancient mystery sought by greedy hands. The boy and girl tell their side of the story, and the honeybees tell theirs in alternating chapters because they can talk too.

Rowan Gordon

Virginia, USA and London, UK

A Lexicon for Bee

Baybee: larval bee
Bitel: beetle
Blodsouker: vampire mite
Brod: brood or tribe
Broder: brother
Cwen: queen
Faeder: father
Feld: field
Forager: field worker
Goldenbrod: Goldenrod's brood
Goldenham: the Goldenbrod hive
Hawbrod: Queen Hawthorn's brood
Humblebee: bumblebee
Hunig: honey
Hyf: hive
Insectors: hive police
King: king
Modor: mother
Mona: moon
Newbie: newborn bee
Noirbitel: ("black beetle") a bee name for Brother Adam

Royal gelee: royal jelly

Smaelbitel: ("small beetle") a bee name for Joe

Steng: sting

Sunne: sun

Sunnedew: the sundew plant

Swuster: sister

Waesp: wasp

Weax: wax

CHAPTER 1

Sting in the Tale

Joe stood behind a table of honey-coloured jars in the shop. He stopped licking his fingers when the bell over the door announced new customers. *Tinkle. Tinkle.*

The head peering around the door wore the most enormous hat he had ever seen. With a broad brim and a dimpled crown, the colour of Devonshire cream, it forced the man to bow under the lintel to enter the abbey shop. He wore blue jeans and a red star on his shirt pocket. The slim woman behind had long blonde hair, dark sunglasses and lipstick the colour of a pillar box. She slung a black leather bag over her shoulder.

Joe watched them approach the counter where his mum straightened her pinafore and combed chestnut curls through fingers.

"Howdy. Y'all still open, Ma'am?" said the large-hatted man.

"You're alright before we close for lunch," replied Mrs. Brawson.

Joe spied on the couple. He tried to place their accent as

they roamed the aisles to glance at merchandise.

The man stopped at a rack of wine bottles to read the label: *Bede's Mead*. The woman almost bumped into Joe, hidden behind a large glossy poster of a gothic building. She slowed to read the title: *Welcome to Oldburgh and its Historic Abbey*. Stopping at the next table, she examined rows of candles moulded from beeswax and assembled like a massed choir of monks.

"Look, Chuck. The Garcias will love one of these Saint Benedicts." She held up a wax effigy of the famous monk with robes dangling at his feet. He had a wick sprouting out of a bald head.

"Jack and Doris are Mormons, Sugar." His grin faded when he gazed around the ceiling. "I'll get that hornet for you, Ma'am."

"I expect you heard my son humming." Joe's mum didn't lower her voice enough to prevent him from hearing. "Other boys tease him about his tic."

"He'll grow out of it," the man said. "I'm Chuck and this is my wife, Becky. We booked for a tour around the abbey and are visiting a castle tomorrow. What's on Friday, Beck?" She didn't reply, too engrossed in a brochure. "We came looking for gifts to take home, but not to exceed the Customs' limit." He gave the wine rack a sour look.

"We sell hive products and loaves from the monastery."

"Mm. I caught a whiff of fresh bread," Becky said without raising her eyes from the page.

"The window picture of your celebrated beekeeper hooked me into your shop," Chuck said. "I've got a whole bunch of hives in my yard outside Dallas. Last year I harvested over two hundred pounds of honey."

"Oh, you're from Dallas! I love that TV series." Mrs. Brawson's face lit up. She reached up to a shelf. "I recommend the latest edition of Brother Adam's book."

"Thanks, but I have one on order at my bookshop since

the old one wore out. Is the brother around? I'd love to meet the man who created the Oldburgh breed. I heard a buzz that he's making an even better bee."

"Sorry to disappoint you. He's giving my Joe a lesson this afternoon, and, unfortunately, his special hive had a setback."

"Sorry to hear that, though your boy will love the hobby. I taught our son, but he prefers fishing."

"Don't tell that story again," his wife snapped.

Joe's ears pricked up.

"I promised Matt a hundred dollars to buy a kayak if he stayed the course. He was *so* scared of getting stung until I cured him. I sat him beside my strongest hive and promised he'd be fine by staying real cool."

They waited for Chuck to stop giggling. "He stayed frozen like a statue for twenty minutes. Guess why?" He couldn't answer his own question until he stopped guffawing.

"Chuck …"

Joe looked at the ticking wall clock. With luck, the chatty American might make them late for his appointment.

"Matt thought I was just giving encouragement when I rubbed his bare arms. He didn't notice I smeared honey on my palms. It didn't take long before they found him after I lifted the hive covers."

Joe cringed. How could a father torture his son like that? His dad taught him to be brave but would be horrified by that prank.

"He found it hard to stay still as dozens of insects tickled his skin." Chuck hooted again. "But they didn't sting him because he wasn't a threat. He's cool walking around my hives now. You never forget a lesson that creeps the bejeepers out of you. Get it: bee jeepers?" The women gave him blank expressions.

"You understand why our son didn't take up beekeeping? Please excuse my husband's sense of humour. He's really a kind person." Becky squeezed his arm, probably embarrassed for not stopping a cruel trial.

Joe wondered if a Yankee boy could suffer under a father's love, how would he fare with a crazy monk who owned a million stinging insects? He stopped humming.

"Joe, come to meet our foreign visitors."

Knowing he couldn't pretend to be absent anymore, he lidded the jar after sucking the last morsel of sweetness. Unfortunately, it wobbled when he tried to balance it on the top row. Lunging to stop it from falling, he knocked over the poster, which brought several jars crashing to the floor. He hung his head to avoid the women's frowns, though the man had a mischievous grin.

"How could you be so clumsy, Joe? Clear them up and be careful if there's broken glass."

He crawled under the table to retrieve rolling jars, grateful for an accident that might delay their departure.

The man sidled over. "Oh boy! Brother Adam's bees will love your sizzling hair and freckles."

Joe barely hid a scowl.

"Bring me a jar, Chuck, to remind us of this visit."

Becky poured coins from her purse and asked how much she owed.

"Two pounds, fifty-three, madam. I'll give you change for three brassy coins." She pressed keys on an antique cash register to close the sale with a sonorous *ding*.

Becky checked her wristwatch. "Oh, my! We'll be late for the antique things we came to see in Oldburgh."

Joe wondered if she meant the abbey or the monk.

"It's not an ancient building," said Mrs. Brawson. "Brother Adam was a novice when the abbey was new, making it about seventy years old. Only the foundations are left from the original abbey that lasted until the reign of King Henry the VIIIth."

"That's the Henry who tore down monasteries and kept

changing wives," said Chuck.

His wife shrugged the hairy arm off her shoulder and showed him the brochure. "Did you know they kept bees here a thousand years ago?"

The question about local history pleased Mrs. Brawson. "The hermit Eadwig was the first beekeeper. There's a legend he was martyred trying to save hives from Viking raiders. Brother Adam believes it's why we have gentle bees today."

"So the bees are paying him back for care they received in the past." The man turned to Joe. "You're a lucky dude to learn from a world expert and will love the flavour of his honey."

He looked at his mum, too timid to speak to a giant. She grinned back, knowing he sampled her jars.

"Do you know it's bee vomit?"

The women waited for him to guffaw again, but only Joe smiled.

"He never stops, even at home," Becky apologised and dug an elbow in her husband's bulging shirt front.

"But it's true, Sugar. Bees drink nectar from flowers like you suck Coke out of a straw. They throw it up when they get back for other bees to turn into honey. Consider that your first lesson, Joe. Call it Beekeeping 101."

Joe liked a man with a sense of humour, unlike the stuffy villagers and poker-faced monks.

"Do you have killer bees where you live, Mister?"

"Sure do. Mean as wolverines. I can't tell the difference between them and my girls until they chase me a quarter of a mile."

Joe's eyes rounded like gobstoppers. "Can they kill you?"

"You betcha. The killers have the same poison as ordinary honeybees. You'll soon know how that feels when you get stung. It's an occupational hazard for beekeepers."

He ignored his wife, who tugged his sleeve to stop alarming the boy.

"Mind you," he continued, "when our Matt joined the marines, he realised a cloud of angry bees is nothing to a war zone."

Joe expected his mum to blanch. She always did when that subject came up. She even banned him from watching war movies.

"I mustn't get stung again," he muttered.

"He should be careful around a hive," his mother butted in to tell the story her way. "He came back from the woods last summer breathing hard with a face all swollen up. I rushed him to the clinic and dreaded to think if a nurse hadn't been around to jab him. She thought it was a wasp."

"Cold-blooded varmints," the man said.

"You must be careful in future. An acute allergy is a medical emergency," Becky said.

"She's a nurse." Chuck pointed at his wife. "But can you be sure it wasn't a bee?"

The grown-ups couldn't tell because most didn't know the difference between a wasp and a honeybee. Joe took extra care to avoid another life-threatening event and the shame of a junior nurse whipping down his pants to jab him on a bare bum. He heard she disliked boys for being taunted as a gypsy girl from a caravan family. So that day, she got revenge on them.

A *dong* on the clock tower reminded them that everyone was running late for their appointments.

"Time for beekeeping, Joe," the man said. "To bee or not to bee, that's the question."

"Quit punning, Chuck, and let these good folks go." Becky pushed her hulking husband to the door. He tipped his Stetson to the shopkeeper and gave the boy a Cheshire cat grin. The shop fell silent after the bell stopped jangling.

Mrs. Brawson flipped the closed sign and hung up her pinafore while Joe stooped to gather more jars. Then, jerked to his feet, he felt her unruffle his mop of hair, so the monk wouldn't think him a scallywag. She fussed about trivial things since there were only two of them at home after losing Joe's father and the pet ferret.

"I don't want to go. What if I get stung?"

"Shame on you. Think what your father would say." She always rolled out that howitzer whenever she lost patience or was in a hurry because he found it hardest to resist. "Brother Adam will teach you safe practices."

"It's not just the bees. I don't want anything to do with him. People will call me a nutcase."

"Don't be rude about your elders. You heard it's lucky to have him as a teacher. And I don't want you messing around with troublemakers and wasting another holiday."

Nothing would sway her after the abbot made arrangements with the monk. Without his dad around, Joe didn't have a reliable ally. He stomped out of the shop, angry to lose precious time on holiday.

Though never introduced to him, he knew the skinny old man as a fixture at abbey services. He wore glasses with thick frames under a thatch that matched his white dog collar. He would parade into the nave among other monks clad in black robes to chant foreign words. A smart aleck in class dubbed them the Abbey Road band for looking like black beetles. Nothing like *the* Beatles.

Brother Adam made rare excursions to the village centre. Joe's former gang snickered openly when they spotted him: "That's the fruitcake who tawks to bees." Even grown-ups thought it wouldn't be long until Brother Adam joined Brother Baldred in the care home. But Mrs. Brawson spoke of him with respect.

One day, Joe saw the monk taking a nap on the garden bench, with his feet up to expose dirty soles in sandals. A kindly lady warned him about bees buzzing around an open honey jar on the table. "Excuse me, sir, but I thought you ought to know—"

She scurried away from the eyes that gave a piercing stare. Joe saw nothing to like about the man who was never seen outside with other monks, except the gardener, Brother Cuthbert. The abbot probably moaned he couldn't do anything about a monk older than the abbey. But on the other hand, shopkeepers were glad if an eccentric monk attracted travellers to their village off the highway. Sometimes, one would drop into the shop to inquire from Mrs. Brawson where they might catch sight of him. They came like ornithologists to tick a rare bird off a checklist.

Mother and son wended through the cloisters to reach the garden. They passed a robed man with his head bowed over a book shaved to a doughnut ring of shaggy hair. No other member of the religious community wore a traditional tonsure.

"Good day, Father Abbot," she greeted him. "We're off to meet the bees."

The abbot hardly raised a hair. Further along the path, Joe twisted around to hold up two fingers at the man who chastened him for stealing a few bitter apples.

She hurried them past visitors huddled on the lawn. When Joe tried dawdling, she tugged forward. A year from his teens, no boy wants to be seen dead holding his mother's hand. But she had to release it as they filed along a narrow path. It bisected a vegetable plot where beans spiralled up poles and cabbages flourished in tidy rows. A monk in a floppy hat stopped hoeing to wave.

"Your garden looks wonderful, Brother Cuthbert." She beamed as the monk plodded in Wellington boots across the sticky loam. Then she dallied out of courtesy to her gentle classmate who, even when they were children, declared he would never marry.

"Our strawberries are almost ready for picking, Mrs. B. Another bumper crop this year, thanks to my brother's pollinators."

"I'll display your punnets in the shop window. Last

year I made jam from surplus berries."

The monk's manner changed as if something troubled him. "I hope the weather lifts your spirits."

A sidelong glance from him was a signal for the boy to withdraw. This was the first time his mum spoke privately to Cuthbert since the funeral.

Joe watched a lark ascending like a helicopter, twittering until level with the abbey tower. His dad had gotten them permission to climb the narrow staircase for the view at the top. Hills hugged the bay to the south, and purple moors crouched under the northern sky. Glad to be praised for not fearing heights, Joe had peered over the parapet to the green copper roof below. It rested on stone blocks thick as a castle wall inside a moat of manicured lawns. The clock in the tower chimed faithfully over the village and across miles of verdant Devonshire countryside. Dad called it the most magnificent landscape in England.

Dropping to his haunches, Joe focussed a magnifying lens on the ground but could still hear his mum nattering to the monk.

"He's still a good lad," she told Cuthbert. "Was youngest in the gang but no longer belongs." He heard the same excuses when she spoke to neighbours over the garden fence. And he blushed when she mentioned his poor grades and that disruptive behaviour sent him to the slow stream after being top in maths. Nevertheless, she insisted he would get on track after a tough year. Nothing could hold her son back when he set his mind on a goal.

Joe hated to have his record broadcast to a gossipy village and guessed what adults thought when they saw him. His mum wanted to convince people she could manage as a single parent and provide the attention he needed. She urged him to make new friends in respectable families. Still, he preferred to keep his own company, mostly roaming the countryside.

He didn't need to excel at school to be a successful adult. Bright boys made it without stacks of certificates. At seventeen, his dad became a Royal Marines commando and earned a commission later without passing school exams. She didn't understand. Nor did Cuthbert judging by his nods, but what did a monk know about life?

"He needs a father figure, Mrs. B. He'll find a soft centre inside the shell when he knows my brother. You'll see the abbot made a wise decision."

"I wish he sent him to you."

"I'm too easy-going for a headstrong lad."

"When Brother Adam is in the shop, he avoids customers asking about his work. He's not a natural teacher, his head too much in the clouds."

"Or in the hives," the monk tittered. "A man of few words, but get him on his favourite topic, and he'll talk the hind leg off a donkey. And no slouch. He's first out of Mass and almost runs back to the bee-yard. I hope I'm as vigorous at nearly ninety. You probably need an obsessive streak to be good at anything, and that's why he's somebody, and I'm still a gardener."

She shook her head to protest. Then, seeing Joe on his knees, she scowled. "What *are* you doing?"

"Blowing up ants," he mumbled. She couldn't see the puffs of smoke from focussing the sun through his lens on an ant trail.

"That's horrid. Ants don't hurt anyone."

"A boy who's fascinated by insects is born to be a beekeeper," said Brother Cuthbert.

"But he murders butterflies and moths, Brother," she replied and shook her head again. "Come on, you scamp. We're keeping Brother Adam waiting."

CHAPTER 2
A New Mutant

The worker bee lifted her head out of the honeycomb to listen. "Did you hear someone tapping feet?" she asked her sister.

"We're behind our deadline for these rows, Daisy. No time for dancing."

The partners clung to the vertical frame with tiny claws alongside other comb-maidens. It would be another wax masterpiece for the queen to lay eggs and nurses to care for baby bees.

Their team worked on frame 2B in the hive nursery, second in a tier of six boxes. The box below had a slit entrance for traffic to fly in and out. Higher storeys served as a pantry for storing honey and pollen. Each contained a dozen frames of comb with rows of cells so straight you might think engineers made them.

Tap. Tap. Tap.

"Surely, you heard it this time?"

"How can you over the din of beating wings?"

Daisy now felt vibrations under her feet. Hyacinth huffed, knowing her sister wouldn't rest until she checked.

She shuffled over to the cluster of cells where baby bees slept under wax caps.

"It came from here."

"Phooey!" Hyacinth remembered the queen coming to lay eggs. She didn't expect births for several more days.

Tap. Tap. Tap. Tap. "LET ME OUT!"

"Bless my feelers," she cried. "You're right. There's someone stuck inside her cell."

Daisy sniffed at the cap with a bendy feeler. "Do you think a baybee is having nightmares?"

"HELP!" The muffled voice sounded desperate. "I'm too cramped to chew the cap open."

The sisters stared at each other. They had never heard of premature birth before, and no honeybee needed a midwife.

"Hold on. I'll get you out in a jiffy."

Hyacinth looked grave as Daisy nibbled the cap. She checked that no one saw her helping a delivery. It was against hive law.

"She will leave a gooey mess if we don't help."

The thought of extra work changed Hyacinth's mind, if grudgingly. But then, she almost jumped out of her cuticle when a feeler poked through a hole. "Watch out, Daisy!"

The slender probe twisted and turned in the air. Daisy

studied a ghostly body writhing under the translucent cap, too intent to notice the patter of feet behind. A voice ordered, "What are you playing at? Get back to work."

She ignored the voice of the despised guard, Pennywort, too absorbed in the spectacle of birth. A head emerged through the enlarged hole. It scanned their faces, and they gawked back.

"Thanks for saving me," the bee said to Daisy. "Can I be your friend?"

Others crowded in behind, curious to see what went on. One barked, "You must be stupid if you think swusters can have friends."

Daisy wouldn't openly defy them. She knew hive lore forbade workers from making favourites in case they formed cliques to share secrets and become uppity. Elite bees might refuse menial jobs and scoff at lower castes. A class system was an abomination.

Instead of equality at all ages, everyone became equalised by promotion in stages. No one stayed at the same level throughout life as worker ants do. They advanced from their first humble jobs to be janitors, nurses, guards, and honey-cooks until finally joining the fleet of revered flyers. It would beggar credibility if every British boy and girl had the right to be a pilot in the Royal Air Force.

Daisy felt torn between the tender appeal of an innocent bee and adhering to a rule she hated. If the hive police broke other laws why couldn't she make a friend? She waited for the newbie to haul out of the nursery cell to preen.

"Phew, that feels better." It rubbed its eyes with a foreleg, its belly with a hindleg, and stretched all four wings to dry.

"Well, blow my spiracles! What in modor's name are you?" Hyacinth snorted through the breathing holes on the sides of her body.

After hearing a kerfuffle, more workers trooped over to ogle a golden bee twice their size and lacking their stripes. The safe arrival of a new baby is usually a cause for celebration, but this one received mixed reactions. Some muttered that a foreign queen had trespassed to secretly lay an egg in their home. Others fell under the spell of her beauty, careless of where she came from. Daisy didn't wait for arguments to settle.

"Welcome to our team of weaxers in Cwen Goldenrod's family. I'm Daisy[47]. This is my partner, Hyacinth[135]. Whatever others may say, you are among friends, so call us by our plant names and drop the numbers."

"Don't be hasty, Daisy," Hyacinth whispered. "She isn't one of us."

"It's a new cwen," someone yelled. "One modor is enough for a hyf; another endangers the peace."

Wings quivered at the prospect of a violent contest. Queen Goldenrod had a gentle reputation, but she wouldn't tolerate a rival.

"Out! Out! Throw it out!" chimed several workers. They had no guilt about eliminating a mutant.

Daisy's voice rose above the clamour as the giant bee, unaware of her peril, continued to remove traces of wax from her body. "Every newbie deserves to be treated as an innocent. You are unjust to banish her without due process. And don't call her 'it' when the alternatives are male or female. A bee without huge eyes can't be a broder, so she must be a swuster, like us."

She continued to defend the newbie. "I admit she's a

rarity and a cwen look-alike, but surely not royal. Cwens are cradled in special cells apart from us. So I will call her a half-cwen until we know better."

The title she just thought up triggered arguments if a hybrid worker-queen could exist. Daisy asked if a label mattered, provided the bee worked hard and stayed loyal.

"You are bonkers," Pennywort declared. "Let me get rid of it."

Daisy didn't easily yield to anger, but she now stood on her hind legs to frantically wave feelers. "You have no authority to ban anyone. The Cwen will hear if you condemn a needed worker."

No one seemed more earnest to get rid of the bee than Pennywort. She snapped that families had always thrived with only three kinds of bees: workers, drones, and a queen. So why accept another, especially a mutant of unproven ability?

Daisy shot back to accuse her of jealousy of someone bigger and stronger. Then Hyacinth calmed the ruckus by suggesting they vote to decide what to do.

"Raise your right feeler if you support the big bee or the left if against."

Daisy held her breath until her side had won a majority. Then she asked who waved more vigorously than others from the back of the crowd.

"You can't mistake Cockscomb. See her legs dusted with red pollen," Hyacinth whispered. "She stalks around recruiting soft-headed swusters to her gang, so don't get pally with her. Now, let me smooth things over."

Hyacinth claimed the crowd's attention as a witness to the birth and from knowing how babies were made.

"Sixteen sunne-days ago, our modor came here to lay eggs," she began in the measured tone of a chronicler. "That's how long it takes to make a new cwen, five days shorter than a swuster and eight fewer than a broder. That could mean the giant bee is a virgin cwen, except for the lack of perfume. Hence, we mustn't rush to decide what kind of bee she is until her nurse explains."

"Well said!" Daisy clapped her wings.

No one wanted to be the nurse of an abnormal birth, so they stayed quiet. Pennywort took the opportunity to retreat on tiptoes, but not quietly enough.

"Why are you sneaking off?" Hyacinth would never dare to challenge a guard unless she had the crowd behind her. "Were you the duty nurse a fortnight ago?"

Still, Pennywort might have ignored the waxer if Captain Cornflower didn't come forward to speak. "I can confirm she left this nursing station to join my unit soon after that date."

The guard didn't risk vexing a senior officer with a denial. She now faced an interrogation because nursing misconduct is a grave offence. No duty is more sacred than the care of baby bees, but that wasn't her only dilemma. She dreaded facing workers after bossing them around and giving punishments for trivial faults. They wanted a scapegoat to avoid blame falling on them.

Hyacinth fired questions like a prosecutor winkling facts and motives out of a prisoner in the dock. Did she overfeed the bee? Did she know the diet fed to larvae made the difference between workers and queens? The defendant fumbled answers and failed to sway listeners or persuade anyone to provide her with an alibi.

She finally admitted to a slipup, though making it sound like a virtue. "No baybee in my care ever went hungry. Is it so evil to give a little extra just to be safe?"

Hyacinth sounded exultant. "Aha! Did all of you hear the admission? Now let's ask if she acted absent-mindedly, which is to say carelessly, or deliberately tried a dangerous experiment to see what happens from overfeeding a baybee?"

Daisy beamed at her brainy partner, sure that she would be fast-tracked for promotion.

Pennywort floundered like a bee spinning on the skin of a puddle. Faces on the unofficial jury were solemn, and the captain didn't throw a lifeline to her underling.

"My head goes fuzzy when the noirbitel smokes us."

The guard's excuse didn't convince anyone. They were supposed to stop work after the keeper smoked the hive until the air cleared.

"I suspect you are hiding something," Hyacinth said. She doubted an extra helping of standard diet would grow a giant worker. "Did you feed her anything else?"

"Just hunig and pollen." Pennywort lowered her eyes.

Casting her memory back to when she was a larva, Daisy recalled her nurse feeding honey for energy and pollen for growth. The tang of royal jelly was a fainter memory. Workers only received a tad of the magical supplement for a few days, whereas future queens gorged on it. They grew faster to become giant bees.

Hyacinth continued to needle her. "Don't try our patience."

Pennywort broke down sobbing, desperate to end the agony. "Perhaps I gave some extra royal gelee to a baybee once or twice."

Hyacinth grinned at her partner, pleased to get to the bottom of the puzzle. But why didn't she own up earlier?

How could she confuse a snug worker cell with a spacious royal booth? Did she play with the fate of an innocent baby?

Daisy shuddered to imagine the disruption if dietary rules were routinely broken. A hive could manage with one exceptional bee if she didn't put on queenly manners. Nevertheless, the giant bee would find it hard to fit into a traditional role in the family.

"You unfaithful swuster!" Hyacinth bellowed. "You gave portions of gelee meant to be shared with other baybees."

"We should tear off her stripes," the captain growled, "but let's not blame the victim."

It pleased Daisy to hear a defence of the newbie. As for the culprit, the jury had no power beyond moral condemnation of an outrageous act. Only the hive police had the authority to punish lawbreakers. When they arrived, Pennywort couldn't expect any mercy from those not belonging to their brood. Pleading sympathy for not covering up her wrong doing with the graver crime of larvicide would be a waste of breath.

"What's up?" The giant bee roused from a snooze to stretch her legs and wings. She felt the noble call to labour so intuitive to bees. "Where do I start working?" She gazed at a circle of faces.

The question pricked the consciences of a crowd who had left their jobs out of curiosity. They hurried back to their workstations before they were caught slacking. Meanwhile, the offender got off scot-free and trotted away with a smirk on her face.

That left Daisy and Hyacinth to decide what to do with the newbie. It seemed kinder to offer security in their team than to let her wander into trouble without friends. Besides, they needed help on their comb, and a mighty bee might make up for the recent loss of two members in their team of twenty-four. So they assigned her to a row of cells that needed scrubbing and remoulding, teaching her to snort fresh wax from glands under her chin.

They didn't take a break the rest of the day except for a short musical interlude. Daisy began singing a famous melody for others to join at intervals and the song to go round and round. All had soprano voices, except a solo alto who sang hesitantly until she got the hang of the tune.

> *Hum, hum, hum as you work,*
> *Mould the weax in your cell.*
> *Busily Buzzily, Busily Buzzily,*
> *Swing feelers and love the smell.*

Heads bowed into cells afterwards. The two partners worked rows on either side of the newbie forging ahead.

Hyacinth whispered to Daisy, "I know you want the big bee to stay, but she needs to be officially approved and have a plant name."

Sooner or later, the police would arrive to certify and name new bees. Daisy dreaded what they would do with a freak, especially now they rejected more bees than before. They claimed a stricter policy raised standards for a healthier family, but how did they decide who was fit to stay? According to rumours, they showed more mercy to bees with stripes like themselves.

"Surely they won't discard an industrious worker. She wants to belong here, and the rest of the team accepts her."

Hyacinth tried to comfort her partner. "We dare not set our hearts on something beyond our control. Enjoy one day at a time and let the future take care of itself."

CHAPTER 3

Cruel and Unusual Punishment

Mother and son followed the garden path to the orchard. Branches and leaves swaying in a light breeze made dappled sunlight dance around their feet. Joe noticed her squinting at apples dangling from the canopy.

"The abbot expects a better harvest this year if boys don't come scrumping."

"Aw, Mum, don't go there again."

The path entered a small graveyard of crosses and headstones crusted with blue-grey lichens, like wafers of Stilton cheese. A rusted iron fence ringed a small mausoleum of white limestone with an oak door. Joe's dad once described a lark he had with schoolmates. Each had to run through the yard in the dark to wake the ghost by knocking on the door. It became a village tradition he wanted his son to do before his teens.

A gate in the ivy-clad wall opened to a meadow and the scent of freshly mown grass. Two dozen grey beehives stood at the far end like an elfin hamlet. Long grass around the hives waited for Cuthbert to come with his scythe. The beekeeper forbade a petrol mower because the noise and draught made the insects frenzied.

They tramped across the turf past a shed with creosote sidings and a slate roof carpeted in moss. A figure swathed in a black robe lolled in a deckchair beside a tall solitary hive. It had sides painted with white doves on a sky-blue background.

A white sun hat and veil lay close by on the grass. A hive smoker reminded Joe of a shiny lamp when he starred as Aladdin in a Christmas panto. He grabbed it. When pumping the bellows didn't make smoke, he dived in his pocket for matches.

"Don't you dare! Put it down!" said his mum. He dropped the tool, though more from aerial bandits closing in than from her scolding. He pranced around, waving arms over his head and told the bees to go away, but it made no difference.

The combination of his yelling and her nagging roused the monk. He didn't conceal an irritation after adjusting the glasses on his nose.

"You're late and have now ruined my nap."

He turned his back to them as Joe did when his mum tugged the quilt off the bed on schooldays. It seemed permission for them to leave, but he knew that look when she pursed her lips. As manager of the monastery shop, she had to stay on good terms with the abbot, who had made arrangements with the monk.

The monk only pretended to doze off again. A muffled voice commanded, "Come back on Wednesday. And be on time!"

Everyone heard that he loathed to chit-chat and chose to communicate in brief chirps like a sparrow to people he hardly knew. This was unsurprising since he became a semi-hermit from long hours in the bee-yard.

Joe inhaled deeply at getting off so easily. Another late start on Wednesday might test the man's patience enough that he might cancel lessons for good. He tried to drag his mother away, but she batted at insects threatening to land on the monk's back.

"Be careful of the bees, Brother."

What did she expect around a hive? Joe huffed at the delay.

The monk turned to give a sly look. He leaned beside the chair to dip a finger in a jar he left open for the insects to enjoy. The bony hand he held out hardly trembled for a man old enough to be Joe's great grandad. The finger commanded attention as a conductor stills an orchestra with a baton before a performance.

It wasn't long until a honeybee landed on the bait. The monk didn't need to utter a word to make his point. Bees treated like pets didn't threaten him, and this one stayed after he touched it tenderly.

"Hello, my golden girl. Are you having a good day?"

So the old man did talk to bees like they said. Joe's mum looked pleased that her son saw them handled as fondly as a piece of cake. It seemed a polished performance as if the adults had planned it to ease his phobia. And in no hurry to leave, she appeared to enjoy watching an intimate moment between the beekeeper and his bees. She could tell customers about the rare privilege of being a witness.

The monk gently blew the insect away. "Tell your boy to come here."

"He's scared of them, Brother."

The monk watched Joe scanning the air like a dove for a hawk. "Anxiety makes you look a fool, boy."

That wasn't the way to win him over. No teacher ever earned a boy's respect by humiliating him. The monk had a reputation for plain speaking and being careless of what others thought. In only that respect, the man and boy were similar. But it didn't matter if they disliked each other. Joe would be out of his hair in the new school year.

"Are you humming, boy?"

Joe ignored a question he suspected a criticism from somebody he hardly knew.

"Don't be scared. Bees are inquisitive creatures and don't bother people who stay calm."

"Remember what the American said, Joe."

Alright for her, he thought, and rolled his eyes. She hadn't noticed bees bombing him, though the monk's grey eyes studied them darting out the entrance slit. Most flew straight as a bullet to the garden, but others buzzed around Joe. He stood stiff as a pole.

"I think they are attracted to you, boy, so you should be grateful."

The man was just as crazy as they said. After waiting all year for the summer holidays, Joe wished he was back at school. The spiteful abbot sent him to a crotchety monk as a lesson. They called him Father Abbot, but there was no more fatherliness in him than a Victorian orphanage boss. Nor did the monk seem to care about his feelings.

"Avoid hairspray and perfume if you don't want them so close."

"He never uses them, Brother," Joe's mum said to defend her son's growing sense of manhood.

"They are attracted to sweetness, so the fruity sweat of a diabetic also excites them."

"He's a perfectly healthy lad. They might smell honey on his hands or something in his pockets." She looked peeved at Joe. "Last week, I found a candy bar in your laundry."

He tapped his pocket to feel the barley sugar twist.

"He's got a sweet tooth like your bees," she said with a big smile.

The joke didn't crack the monk's face, as glazed as a porcelain vase.

"We saw smaller hives lower down in the meadow. They might be better for training novices than this strong hive."

The monk took a deep breath, like an expert unable to comprehend general ignorance. Joe felt sorry for his mother, who had good intentions.

"One day, Mrs. B, every novice will train with this gentle breed. I didn't name the queen Peacemaker for nothing, but if he wants a sterner challenge—"

The monk stopped at something rousing his attention. He got out of the chair to examine the boy from all directions. On feeling the back of his T-shirt tugged, Joe turned to see the monk open a clenched hand to release a couple of bees. He looked wide-eyed at his mum.

"If you hadn't stopped behaving like a jack-in-a-box, they might have pricked to let you know they were there. Humming might have helped. It's a good habit for a beekeeper to soothe them like the positive karma of a Buddhist monk."

Joe thought it was a strange comparison for a Catholic monk to make, though he got the point. He had seen saffron-robed Vietnamese monks on telly. They sat frozen with crossed legs and far away looks as they hummed a mantra: *AUM—AUM—*

He often hummed to himself, unaware of the habit until the boy beside him in class dug an elbow in his ribs. His mum thought it stopped him fidgeting with a book or his insect collection. Unfortunately, she started blabbing about that hobby.

"You ought to see his collection. He spends hours arranging pretty butterflies with neat labels. Brother Cuthbert thinks he's a natural beekeeper."

The monk folded his brow. "I thought boys gave up butterfly collecting a long time ago. This isn't a place for anyone who kills pollinators. Does he rob bird nests too?"

Words spoken so deliberately sounded like condemnation for a mortal sin. She turned crimson and denied that her son ever stole an egg. The monk wafted a bee from Joe's shoulder to break an awkward silence.

"I wonder why you attract them."

"I mustn't get stung again!" He sighed to let his mum explain.

"He had a bad wasp sting last year. The abbot said it doesn't mean he's allergic to bees."

She looked at the monk for confirmation but should have known he wouldn't contradict a superior.

"I assure you, Madam, they only sting as a last resort because it's fatal for them. But not all bees can sting. I learned that at his age at the circus. What are you leering at, boy?"

Joe wiped his smile but couldn't get rid of a funny

picture. He imagined the monk in the stalls watching brontosauruses parade nose to tail under the Big Top.

"A man coming into the ring held a jar under the big nose of a clown that dashed away," the monk began, keeping a straight face. "It was full of bees, but not many escaped before he poured them into his mouth. As he staggered around with pursed lips and swollen cheeks, we thought he must be insane."

Joe's mum cringed, no doubt to remember how a single sting on his leg caused a reaction that squeezed his windpipe and gave him nightmares for weeks. She probably wondered why the monk would scare the boy, though no one learns to be tactful from a life of solitude. Still, his childhood memory showed him loosening up on a subject he cared about. Just as Cuthbert said, there was more to him than the crabby public image.

"The performer with bloated cheeks held us in suspense," the monk continued, "until opening his mouth to let them fly out. The act ended with a bow and a grin. Grown-ups debated if he used a conjuring trick or coated his mouth with a repellent. I stayed to look for clues in the interval."

The monk paused, probably thinking he had them stumped for an answer. Joe wouldn't let him get the better of them. He knew only one likely explanation for the trick and let it dribble out in an offhand way. "He used drones because they can't sting."

His mum beamed when she saw the monk raise his eyebrows. "He knows more about bugs and creepy-crawlies than anyone and will soon get used to your bees. I expect the circus man felt scared at the first performance," she said.

"Aw, Mum, you don't know what you're talking about."

"Precisely, Mrs. B. It's about familiarity. Perhaps I can make something of your boy if he doesn't waste time pussy-footing. When he gets used to checking this hive, I'll let him do weekly inspections for the rest. I need a backup if I fall ill."

Joe turned a shade of grey as his outlook suddenly worsened. Walking to the shed, he noticed a gleam in the monk's eyes, confirming a suspicion the monk wanted an assistant from the arrangement, even if the abbot had different intentions. He kicked himself for not playing a worthless fool, so the monk would wash his hands of him.

He snuck inside the shed behind their backs while they talked about restocking the shop after the honey harvest. The air had the sweet and waxy aroma of honeycomb. Tools on the bench tempted him to rummage since he wasn't allowed in his dad's tool chest. A pale-yellow bottle like those in the shop rack caught his notice but a skinny arm snatched it away before he could pull the loose cork.

"Leave my tonic alone, boy!"

"What got into you, Joe, first tampering with his tools and now the drink?"

He avoided his mum's glare.

The monk took a jar from a cupboard. "You don't deserve a reward and must earn it next time."

Joe lowered his eyes as he poked out his tongue for honeycomb, like the wafer his mum received from the priest at the altar rail. Honey dribbled down his chin as he chomped the soft wax. He couldn't refuse it, even knowing the monk gave it as a down payment on future help. He said a silent prayer for rain on Wednesday, although that first day in the yard ended better than expected. He started to leave, but she stalled again.

"Would you mind if his cousin Emily joins the lesson? She's a sensible sixteen-year-old staying with us for the holidays."

Joe groaned. He had mentally prepared for Emily swanning around the house but hadn't suspected his mum had invited her to be a chaperone for him. He guessed the monk wouldn't allow a girl in his precious yard, so he was shocked when told that beekeeping wasn't just for men and boys. The monk even offered a spare bee suit for her but had no protective clothing in a boy's size. Mum offered to make Joe a coverall and veil with a see-through screen, which the monk said should be a white fabric that doesn't excite bees.

"I'll dust off my *Singer* sewing machine, Brother, to sew an outfit from an old bed sheet and spare lace from my wedding dress."

"Aw, Mum, don't do this to me!" She made her son feel like a little kid again.

His mum instructed him to go straight home to greet Emily, who had booked a ticket on the midday express from Paddington. After several years apart, he wondered if she was a hoity-toity city girl.

Riding along the High Street on his mountain bike, he passed a postman emptying a pillar box and a bus growling at a stop. To avoid a swarm of tourists, he turned down a gravel lane between thatched cottages where thick tyres bumped over ruts and spat grit. He romped homeward on a sugar high, glad to be free.

Further down the lane, someone stood astride a red bike as a patrol car might block the traffic. Brad Grattich! Joe slowed to a crawl. Tough luck to be caught on his patch after evading him since the abbot's inquisition.

He screeched to a halt and resisted the temptation to turn around as the other boy rode up in a leather jacket and dyed purple hair. Brad looked taller than last time and had a new shadow over his lip.

"Where yer been, Ginge?"

"Messing about." Joe tried to look casual.

"I heard yer were 'elping the gaffer who tawks to bees."

He couldn't deny it. Gossip spreads like wildfire in a little village.

"Yore becoming a right 'oly Joe. Do yer want to be a monkey like them?" The sneer conveyed contempt for the monastery that the Grattich family was known for.

"I 'ad no choice cos the abbot wanted someone to blame." Joe slipped into gang lingo without realising.

"We don't 'ave a good climber since yer deserted us."

The gang depended on Joe for roguery in orchards and houses. He had once let them into a derelict house by shimmying up a drainpipe to enter a broken window on the second floor. After opening the front door for them, the older boys carted off the good stuff, not that he wanted any of it. Earning their praise was all the reward he wanted.

"Yer should 'ave kept yer gob shut about the orchard

job when the boss monkey asked."

"I never split on yer!"

He didn't feel wicked for telling fibs to Brad and never intended to give them away. The abbot forced him to confess while his mum sat quietly as a mouse. He took the blame for the greed of others and only managed to scrump a couple of apples before getting caught.

The others tore down branches to snatch the ripest fruit and bunked him up trees for throwing those out of reach to catchers below. The gang would have stripped the orchard before harvest time if a monk hadn't come along and found Joe stranded like a goose on a high bough. They deserted him and sold the goods to a greengrocer in the next village. He didn't receive a penny or show it rankled.

"Why bother me? No one else got punished."

"But we worry about our reputation, kiddo." He laughed at his own joke. "My Pa sent the boss monkey off with a flea in 'is ear for accusing me of being a raider. Little snitches don't deserve to be let off, but I'll overlook the fault for a bottle of yer old woman's 'oney wine. She won't miss it."

Joe dreaded a meeting that couldn't be avoided forever, and now it put him in a quandary. Which was worse: to break his mum's iron rule of honesty or inflame the gang leader's temper?

"She'll kill me if I steal it."

"Don't yer want to 'elp an ole friend?" He grabbed a yank of Joe's hair. "Better dead than red."

What did that mean? To submit to threats would put him under Brad's power. Then the bully could expose him as a thief the next time they fell out, making the last trouble worse than the first.

Twisting his head still under the grip, Joe saw another boy riding up and light a cigarette.

"Got a spare, Pete? I'm skint."

"I can't pinch any more this week."

"Then gimme a drag and I'll share the bottle this young offender is getting for me."

"Let me go. My mum's expecting me." Joe regretted making a feeble appeal when Brad wrenched his head back. Pete blew smoke in his eyes.

"Hum, hum," Pete mocked Joe's habit. "You don't look 'appy to see us, Ginge. Are yer feeling guilty?"

He had to get away from the two meanest kids in the gang before he suffered more torment. With the incident over the monk's bottle still fresh in his mind, he had a suggestion that might get him off the hook and didn't care about the consequences. "The monk keeps a bottle in 'is shed. I got caught with it today, so it's up to you to get it when 'e gocs to midday prayers."

"Don't lie to me or I'll track yer down." Brad kicked Joe's wheel with a leather boot. "Yer won't get far on this crappy bike." He exchanged a laugh with Pete. "The Brawsons are all losers. Their granddad wouldn't stand up to mine, and 'is old man copped it fighting on that island full of sheep and seagulls. How stupid is that?" Pete sniggered in agreement.

Joe remembered his parents arguing about a war in the Falkland Islands before his dad was deployed there. His mum begged to know if they were worth saving.

Brad pointed at a pair of crows flapping over a patch of woodland they called a spinney. "My Pa could blast them with both barrels at once. If yer dad were a better shot, 'e might still be around and not pushing up daisies where sheep piss on 'im."

Brad didn't see the fury about to boil over from insulting the honour of his victim's hero. He deliberately turned a knife in Joe's emotional wound, knowing what happened to Mr. Brawson, as everyone did who heard the news.

A tall girl appeared further down the lane but too far away to see the clashing boys. When Brad released his grip,

Joe leaned down to examine the spokes of his wheel. When he came upright again, the beeswax pellet had moved from inside his cheek to behind his lips. A straight shooter from practising with plum stones, he stared the beefier boy in the face. Then taking a deep inspiration, he blew out with hurricane force. The bullet hit Brad in the eye, making him reel in shock and tumble over Pete.

Joe had a head start while the enemy dried his eye. With a pounding heart, his feet blurred on the pedals. Brad climbed on his racer to give chase with gritted teeth on a face the colour of a raspberry stain.

CHAPTER 4
Hail the Sunne

Daisy roused her partners. "Wake up, you sleepy heads! Feldbees have already gone out to forage."

Hyacinth yawned through her spiracles. "Is it that time already? I wanted a long snooze after the hubbub made us work late yesterday."

"You can't laze here all day. I'm taking her for a quick tour."

Hyacinth huffed. "We'll get further behind the schedule if you both skip off."

"I promise to catch up. Remember, our new recruit isn't a loafer."

That made the newbie smile, who needed to be nudged to leave work. Daisy wanted private time together. "We say life is about work, but it's no sin to take a quick view from the top of the hyf."

They climbed up a dark corner of the wall, hoping to avoid guards who might question an odd-looking bee. She bombarded Daisy with questions about the sounds and smells pervading the hive that were new to her.

"What's that whirring sound?"

"Honey-cooks are fanning cells to dry nectar for making honey."

"Is that bland odour from a different food?"

"You probably smell pollen turning into bee bread."

"There's something else I can't describe, except as a happy scent."

"The aroma of weax and honey masks most things. I guess you mean a whiff of Queen Goldenrod's perfume. We dread what would happen to us without it."

At the next storey, they met comb-maidens topping up cells with nectar from wildflowers. A group of foragers hung around a waggle dancer. She took several steps forward, then curved back before going forward again to complete a figure of eight. The newbie had never seen dancing like that before.

"Don't think she is wasting time or dancing just to entertain them. Her steps point to a patch of dandelions which she is advertising with a ditty." They tapped feet to her humming:

> *Hive-ho, Hive-ho*
> *We're off to flowers I know.*
> *Clover, daisies, and savoury chive*
> *Make tasty honey for our hive.*

Hive-ho, Hive-ho
Come to the garden show.
Watch my feet do a little jig
They point you to a nectar swig.

Daisy hustled them away before a guard questioned the outsized bee. They hadn't gone far when they had to stop for a coughing fit. A voice from a higher storey cried repeatedly:

"SMOKE-ALARM! SMOKE-ALARM . . . !"

It triggered a roar from thousands of feet bolting to lower storeys. The pair waited until the stream reversed direction a few minutes later.

"Is the panic over?" Daisy asked an old bee at the end of a line.

"The noirbitel puffed smoke from its firebox. Not to

worry, but you shouldn't breathe the unhealthy air."

After the all-clear, the pair continued to a place Daisy had visited before. On that occasion, the top covers blocked the view, but now she hoped to be lucky before the keeper closed the hive after an inspection.

Sunlight poured into the box to briefly blind them. They waited until it was safe to crawl along the ridge of a frame for a panoramic view of the Wide World.

Neither of them imagined a world so beautiful. Puffy white clouds marched across the blue arc of heaven. A golden orb dangled by an invisible cord, shining so fiercely it forced them to look away.

"Sunne is the modor of everyone," Daisy said, still lowering her gaze. "The world would be a barren desert without her." Besides the sun, a pale white crescent was suspended from the sky, not so well-known since it wasn't present every day. "Mona is not so great as Sunne, although moths worship her for lighting the night."

They clambered along the narrow parapet, planting feet prudently to avoid wobbling. As they hadn't flown yet, they couldn't be sure of saving themselves if they fell.

They paused for an enchanting view of the green landscape decorated with flowers and blossoms of every colour. Bees can see the blue end of the rainbow spectrum better than humans but the red end poorly. However, they perceive a deep purple invisible to humans that some plants use for attracting pollinators. Despite the blessing of colour vision, the partners' feelers gave the greatest pleasure from detecting molecules drifting from floral bouquets in distant fields.

Continuing to stroll, they spied flyers at the entrance below. Above the slit, a brown mat of bees cooled in the shade after working in hot fields.

"We will fly like them one day," Daisy said. "Think how many places we will see together."

"I can't imagine anywhere better than basking here in Sunne's rays."

Daisy was also tempted to linger for the panorama, but they ought to return to Hyacinth. Soon after beginning a descent, the sky switched from blue to black. A pink claw reaching out of the murk nearly touched the newbie.

Daisy watched in horror as her friend dodged the claw by zigzagging on the parapet. A misstep tripped the newbie over the edge, but luckily falling inside she could dive to safety between frames. Daisy followed on surer footholds because the claw didn't lunge at her. The pair peeped out of their hiding place when sunbeams poured down again. Although feeling relief after the threat retreated, the giant bee had exposed herself to suspicious eyes on a comb where neither of them were known.

"Don't worry, she's in my team," Daisy assured them. "Do you know who tried to attack her?"

"You are green bees if you haven't seen a bitel before," a worker snickered. "They are the weirdest four-legged creatures you are ever likely to meet. They use two legs to walk on and have a spare pair hanging loose. Our noirbitel is one of that kind and unmistakable with a black carapace and white head. It comes babbling in a strange language and pouring smoke but not aggressively. I don't know why it chased your friend."

"You will meet unfriendly bitels outside when you qualify to fly," another worker warned. "They might bash your wings from thinking you are a waesp. And take care around those on all-fours because they have a fifth leg used as a nasty whip at the rear. There's also a chilling story about one with a striped face. It breaks into hyfs to gobble everything in reach, including baybees."

"Did the noirbitel want to eat me?"

The workers laughed at the newbie. "Don't be daft. It's not carnivorous. It takes some of our hunig to eat in its stone hyf, but Sage says we shouldn't grumble because it brings candy in winter. She thinks Sunne sent it to take care of us."

"Who's Sage?"

"Does your big friend know anything?" she asked.

Daisy would have explained about the eminent bee if the chatterbox didn't hog the conversation.

"I've seen a swuster taking a ride on the noirbitel's claw," the second bee continued. "She claimed it had two eyes instead of five and a pink flap on each side of its head for feelers. I'm amazed it can survive without better sight and smell."

"It's usually alone, but today it brought a smaelbitel that hummed one of our favourite tunes," said the first bee. "Treat them as friends who don't deserve to be stung."

Daisy tapped her friend with a feeler. They shouldn't stand jabbering there all day.

They hurried back to join Hyacinth and the rest of the team on their comb. It wasn't toiling to work alongside friends who shared stories and sang together. They hummed like cogs in a well-oiled machine, not planning a break until field bees came home for the night. But voices counting numbers made them stop to listen.

"65, 66, 67 . . ."

Daisy gasped when she realised. "Oh blimey, it's

Hemlock and her flunkeys. You can tell by their stripes they belong to the late Cwen Hawthorn's brood." She had no time to explain why another brood lived in their hive or if it mattered.

Hyacinth had a grave face. "There's no telling what the Chief Insector will do if she sees our new friend."

If the police decided to interrogate the newbie, she couldn't look for support from Captain Cornflower. Guards protected the family from enemies coming to steal from hives. The police battalion, on the other hand, served as the community law-keepers with the power to punish lazy or naughty bees. Woe betides those caught on the wrong side of the chief of police.

"Leave this to us," Daisy advised the giant bee. "If she grills you, be polite and don't call Hemlock by that nickname. She likes to be addressed as the Chief. The other two are deputies, Nightshade and Skunk Cabbage. We invented those names too, shortened to Shady and Skunkie behind their backs."

"What funny names."

"Not funny at all when you know them. We named two after poisonous plants and the third from the fragrance of a smelly plant. But, hush, they're almost here."

The three law-keepers strode forward side by side and

swung their legs in unison.

"What a pleasant surprise, Chief." Hyacinth stepped forward as if greeting a respected friend. "If you came on urgent business, will you take refreshments first?"

Hemlock sneered at the pretence of courtesy. "You were supposed to finish this comb by sunne-set yesterday. We saw several messy rows and team members scuttled away when they saw us coming."

"They are meeting to discuss a new method for boosting efficiency, called acme waxing. You can ask Daisy." The partners agreed to back each other up with excuses when officials made unreasonable demands. Hemlock looked mistrustful, having been fooled by wily Goldenbrods before.

"Take the names and numbers of these goons, deputy."

Shady saluted with a feeler. "Yes, boss. Did you mean only this pair or include the fat bee trying to hide?"

"I'm not blind, you oaf."

Hemlock demanded from Hyacinth a progress report and rattled off a series of questions. When would they finish the job? Did they check for straight rows? Had they cleared it of poison from the fields? And so on. After earning respect as chief investigator for the birthing inquiry yesterday, Hemlock humiliated Hyacinth as if she was a shyster. Daisy came to her rescue.

"We aren't laggards, Chief. We need help to finish the comb by the closing date or work ourselves to death."

"Do you think you're smarter than comb managers who are trained to calculate how many workers we need to deploy to a comb? Let's see how well you perform at maths." Hemlock turned to ask Shady, "What are the dimensions of this comb?"

"I counted forty-eight cells wide by eighty long, boss."

"You heard that, weaxer? Now, multiply to give me the total number of cells." Hemlock grinned at the deputy. "You can't expect their kind to know time's tables. They have a ganglion in their head instead of a brain."

Daisy didn't want to let her brood down with a mistake, but the calculation befuddled her. Never learning past twelve times in class, forty-eight times was a far greater magnitude than she attempted. It helped to use the trick of transferring the nought from the eighty to the forty-eight to reduce the multiplier to a manageable number eight. When her head began to spin, she hazarded a guess to avoid giving Hemlock the satisfaction of defeating her.

"Three thousand cells."

"She's wrong, boss." Shady thought she had the answer. "It's three thousand five hundred."

"Why was I given charge of so many gormless insects?" Hemlock huffed. "Neither of you are management material if you can't do simple arithmetic. The correct number is four thousand." She repeated with a raised voice: "FOUR THOUSAND."

She took their smiles as compliments, not realising they were disguised expressions of pleasure to see Shady share the humiliation. Then a low voice behind Daisy made heads rubberneck to see who spoke.

"That number is too high."

The newbie couldn't allow an error to pass without comment, although she only intended to make Daisy feel better after being ridiculed. But with all eyes turned on her, she felt bound to give an answer, and blurted out, "I calculate three thousand eight hundred and forty cells on this comb. However, we ought to adjust for damage on the top row. In that case, it reduces the total to three thousand seven hundred and ninety-two."

After a silence, Shady looked at her boss. "That can't be right."

"Shut up, deputy. You already proved you're no genius." Hemlock scanned the faces in Daisy's team. "Tell me, and don't be shy, who you think is the better mathematician: this chunker or me?"

Faces looked around, hoping someone else would break the silence. It fell to Daisy to make a brave appeal. "You could be right, Chief, but please don't give her a hard time. The big bee was only born yesterday and is still learning hive manners. We never saw a more handsome or brainy bee in the hyf."

A glare meant she had made a blooper for offending Hemlock's vanity. Daisy wished she had her partner's diplomacy with words, but the ugly moment passed when Shady butted in.

"What shall we do with an ugly mutant who pretends to be a queen, boss?"

"You know the penalty for impostors."

"We feed them to the birds."

The prospect of capital punishment drew a small crowd curious to know the giant's fate. Belonging to the newbie's brood, they had voted to save her yesterday but now stood as timid spectators in the police presence.

"Give it a thorough examination," Hemlock sniffed. "I want to know what kind of bee it is and the nurse responsible."

Daisy winced at the impersonal pronoun, *it*. Those two letters were used to describe her friend as an object of derision when she was a subject of the realm by birthright.

Shady tapped the newbie's body to listen for the hollow sound of air sacs needed for sustained flight and then flipped the valves to check breath control. She measured the length of the sting's shaft, the clarity of eyes, the bendiness of feelers, and much else. She groaned, hoping a thorough examination of the wings would reveal a fault.

"They are too short for take-off with a full cargo of pollen," she declared with glee.

Honeybees don't stay inside their hive as pedestrians forever. When they become foragers, they need strong wings to carry food over several miles. Other insects chortled at their tiny wings for their body size. But bees compensate with muscles that can beat extremely fast, like powerful engines that jumbo jets need to get aloft. No one could be sure whether the newbie had the strength to overcome gravity until the test flight.

"Hmm. That's a fatal flaw. Why didn't a nurse squelch the mutant before birth? Don't keep me waiting for an answer." Hemlock's stern countenance tried to intimidate someone in the crowd to admit making a mistake or betray another bee.

Finally, a junior bee broke down to declare what she had seen. "Pennywort admitted she fed extra royal gelee to make a giant."

"In that case, we don't need to pursue our inquiries further. I spend too much time chasing swusters from your brod failing their duty," Hemlock growled.

She instructed Skunkie to scour the boxes until she found the offender for escorting her out of the hive. Serious crimes used to be considered by a careful jury, but, lately, punishments were meted out without due process, called summary justice. Police attitudes had hardened after the keeper installed Goldenrod as the new queen. She had rehired officers from the previous regime of Cwen Hawbrod until breeding her own, hoping they would act reasonably and responsibly. Although pledging loyalty, they secretly held grudges against her brood and none felt more aggrieved at the hive take-over than Hemlock.

"We don't tolerate faults that upset society," said Hemlock. "There are sacred rules for making queens. I will expel anyone who tries to cheat, not only villains like Pennywort but fraudulent queens they create with illegal gelee."

"Please listen, Honorable Chief." Daisy hated the title of a despised official, but she had to grovel to save a bee in peril whom she secretly regarded as a friend. "We harm our family if we waste a prize bee innocent of a crime and eager to work. I beg you to let her prove herself."

The giant bee had let Daisy speak for her so far, but now she understood the stakes after they sentenced the guard. "Please don't send me away. It's too soon to end my story."

Hemlock paced up and down to decide what to do. Pleas for mercy had never moved her before, so an act of clemency flummoxed them and even surprised Shady.

"Ahem." Hemlock cleared her spiracles with a cough. "You know I love our commonwealth, this peaceful and productive community. You have seen me slow to anger, swift to praise, a lover of mercy . . ."

Everyone felt obliged to listen to the baloney, and no one dared to laugh. As Hemlock continued her oration, Daisy thought the dramatic change of attitude must be a smokescreen for those who didn't know her brutal record.

"In the past, we treated mutants as potential troublemakers, but let's judge by behaviour and not from physical differences. Most insectors wouldn't let this oddball off, so it had a lucky day when I came along."

The newbie danced around. "Thank you, Chief. I won't let you down."

The bystanders raised their feelers in salute. Whatever they thought of the police chief before, it seemed an omen for better times between the quarrelsome broods. Daisy's appeal had only apparently softened a hard heart.

"Of course, I can't let a mutant off scot-free without checking." The chief faced the newbie. "We need to see if you have the endurance to belong here. It's not a cushy life as a working swuster. But a strapping bee should sail through a test, and I will make it easier by giving you a choice. You can spend a day and night outside or in a snug apartment reserved for special guests in the bottom box. Then, if all goes well, you can return to ordinary duties with your team."

No one ventured to challenge Hemlock about why an almost flawless bee should be put through an ordeal. Daisy suspected the chief played with the trust of an innocent bee because it wasn't in her nature to flip-flop. Was it a ruse to get rid of her? If so, she wouldn't be the first to go missing, but there was no official review of what happened to them. So which option was the least awful? Threats abounded outside at night, whereas the risks were unknown in the dark box below.

They hadn't noticed Cockscomb in the crowd until she yelled, "Don't be fooled by talk of a cosy cell. The Cryptum is a diabolical place."

Although known for outrageous views, the warning couldn't be discounted. Cockscomb had resigned from her comb to roam for information about the Disappeared.

Hemlock didn't want a slanging match that might publicise what the rebel had learned, so she chose honeyed words to reassure the newbie.

"Trust me as a caretaker of our family, not those who want to tear down authority. Instead of punishment, regard your choice as a challenge to prove you are a special bee."

"If I go outside, I will be remembered for being treated like a criminal," said the newbie, "so I must choose the Cryptum instead."

Cockscomb stomped off, shaking pollen off her wings in disgust. The display made Daisy anxious because she, too, thought the other option was better. Moreover, she could sneak outside to keep her friend company after dark.

"So be it," declared the chief with a solemn face. "Now let us gather around for a ceremony to certify you. Repeat the oath after me: I promise to work hard and serve my family loyally to the end of my days, so help me, Sunne."

Daisy's team congratulated the newbie on becoming a member of the sisterhood.

"Not so fast, comrades," Hemlock commanded them with a raised feeler. "We aren't finished until a newbie is given a plant name. A rare bee can't have a common name like a daisy." She turned from Daisy to Shady. "Do you have a suggestion, deputy?"

Surprised to be asked, Shady offered the first name coming into her head. "What about Fool's Parsley?"

Hemlock chuckled at the mockery, not realising it was a poisonous plant closely related to her nickname. But she had already decided and never took her squad seriously in case they became ambitious above their station.

She raised a feeler over the bee's head: "From henceforth, I pronounce you Sunnedew. Don't let me catch anyone calling you a big bee again."

Sundew's head went into a spin. She did a jig to celebrate a unique name and, therefore, a number one in an extraordinary reversal of fortune. "Thank you for the honour, Chief. It fulfils a dream I had as a baybee cradled in my cell in which I visited flowers glistening with dew in the sunneshine."

Her two friends stood aloof, not jealous of a name nobler than theirs but puzzling about what it meant. Cold feelings melted after they opened cells of vintage honey for a toast. After a few sucks, Daisy took Sundew aside.

"Your classy name will be the talk of the hyf, but I want to call you Dewy."

"I can't shorten your name, Daisy, but I will drop the forty-seven because you will always be a number one to me."

Hyacinth departed with the crowd, leaving Daisy to watch two guards escorting Sundew to the Cryptum. She sat musing about all they had heard until a foul odour distracted her.

"Keep your distance. You should hang your head in shame for not giving Pennywort a proper hearing before a a magistrate for a capital crime," she told Skunkie.

"We all do our duty. Why should you care about her, who never did anyone a favour?"

Daisy snorted, unable to answer. "You missed the ceremony for investing Sunnedew as a swuster. It's a funny name that no one has heard of." She assumed the stooge didn't know or wouldn't tell. "They are taking her to the Cryptum. Does that place ring a bell? Don't hide it from me, or I'll come after you when Hawbrods are a minority and we have new insectors."

Skunkie pondered over her loyalties. She presently sheltered under Hemlock's power but would have more security in future as the new brood grew in number.

"You know how hard solitary confinement can be on our emotions, but there's something worse. The Cryptum is called the tomb of the living dead. No bee has come out alive except as a zombie drained of blood."

Struck with horror, Daisy begged for more information.

"It is the redoubt of vampire blodsoukers that wait patiently for bee prisoners."

"Sunne forbid! What are they like?" Daisy had boundless terror of bloodsucking mites.

"They are minute, eight-legged spiders. Although blind and deaf, they stalk their prey by scent instead of trapping them in cobwebs."

"So why haven't the guards overpowered them if they are tiny?"

"When they first arrived, we chased them into the vault but didn't dare go further. We could have sealed the devils inside to starve them to death, but our bosses decided to make a pact. For promising to stay inside, the mites were rewarded by feeding them with live bees."

"Crikey! So that's what happened to disappearing bees. They were executed and we weren't even given their corpses for proper burial. But I don't worry about Sunnedew, who is big enough to take care of herself."

Skunkie lowered her head. "Their horny shells are too tough to be pierced with a sting or jaws."

Daisy jumped up to run after the squad, unable to bear more details.

CHAPTER 5
Has Joe got Talent?

Joe steered floating Cheerios around his breakfast bowl. He hadn't touched the toast or tasted the apple juice when his mother came into the room scowling.

"I don't want him coming to the shop complaining about you again. You're not skipping another lesson. Besides, Emily is eager to learn about beekeeping."

"Aw, Mum, there was no point going on Wednesday because bees hate getting wet."

"It only drizzled, and Brother Adam waited in the yard for ages."

They both turned to the sound of footsteps on the staircase as Emily came down.

"He's almost ready, dear, and lost his appetite. But, hey, you look dressed for a party."

Emily wore a floral blouse tucked inside white slacks. A stylist had trimmed her chestnut hair like Princess Diana's at last year's royal wedding.

"I could only carry a small trunk on the train and didn't expect to hang out in a bee-yard. Is the monk weird?"

"Make up your mind about Brother Adam instead of

listening to an opinionated boy." She gave him a dirty look.

After her aunt returned to the kitchen, Emily wandered around the dining room to gaze at framed portraits. She paused at the photograph of an army officer saluting a platoon and asked, "Is that my Uncle Gordon?"

Joe pushed the bowl aside. "They made Dad a lieutenant that day."

"Do you want to be a soldier when you grow up?"

"Over my dead body!" his mother said, coming to clear the table. "He's going to college to study farming or something else useful."

Emily whispered, "Can you show me the medal? My mum said it ought to be kept at the bank, but she thinks it's still here."

He led her upstairs, checking from the landing they weren't followed. He dropped to his knees in his mother's room and pulled out an old trunk from under her bed.

"That's not a safe place," she said.

Joe found a trinket box buried among old clothes and bundles of letters. Opening it revealed a bronze cross cradled in blue silk. He dangled it on a crimson ribbon from his fingers before lowering it to her palm. Emily read aloud the pithy inscription he knew under the lion and crown: *For Valour.*

"I'm surprised it's not made of gold, and the words don't seem enough," she said. "You know my parents went with your mum to the palace reception? Dad said if she sold the medal at auction, it could pay off her mortgage.

"She's keeping it for me one day," Joe said.

Dishes clinked in the kitchen sink as the cousins crept downstairs, pretending they had never left the room. His mother reappeared, wielding a flyswatter.

"I don't know how they get indoors." After chasing a bluebottle around the room, she stopped to catch her breath and reminded Joe to take the outfit she made. She gave him a pat on the head and Emily a kiss on the cheek as they went out the door.

Joe walked ahead in case classmates thought they were together. However, he fell back to be glad of her company at the High Street where two louts lolled against the Post Office wall.

"Oh, blimey! They mustn't see me."

Emily grabbed his wrist to stop him from turning back. "You never told me why they chased you, but they can't hurt you in a public place."

"You don't know them," he said, prising off her fingers.

"They won't see you if you put the veil on."

Joe hesitated to look that idiotic until she insisted it would work. He had only worn the outfit before when his mother cut a letterbox opening for a lookout that showed little of his face. He felt like a scared rabbit wrapped in a blanket. Tripping on the kerb, he refused the hand she offered. The youths hooted and wolf whistled as they marched past on the other side of the street.

"Hey, gorgeous. Is the phantom taking you out for an early 'alloween date?"

What would they do if they whipped off his cover? Joe looked steadily ahead with ears pricked for footsteps. The youths didn't cross the street, already satisfied by making catcalls, and Emily's killer scowl may have made the passage safer. Joe took a deep breath when the voices faded.

Would his father call him chicken if he saw him now or laugh his head off? Duping the boys reminded him of a bedtime story about soldiers disguised under sheepskins to spy on an enemy camp. Dad called them wolves in sheep's clothing.

He felt better from tearing off the veil at the monastery entrance. Still, the relief only lasted to the meadow gate from where they saw the monk standing outside the shed.

As hostile eyes focussed on the boy walking up, Emily whispered, "I expected him to look like a saintly Francis of Assisi or jovial Friar Tuck, but he's as bony as my Latin teacher."

"Did she drag you here, boy?" the monk asked with a granite face. "I've got a bone to pick with you."

Joe prepared to be dressed down for missing a lesson, although the man looked more severe than he deserved. The reason became clear when Brother Adam held out a bottle from behind his back and turned it upside down. Not even a drop came out.

"Recognise it? After taking it from the shed, you threw it in the grass where someone could trip on it."

Joe covered his mouth. Brad had taken the wine, but the dodge boomeranged back on him. He would get killed for grassing on the bully, but keeping his mouth shut would be an admission of guilt to the monk. *I'm damned if I do and damned if I don't.*

"Excuse me, sir, there's something you should know." Emily addressed the monk formally after being ignored. To call him Brother Adam seemed too familiar for a man of great antiquity. Joe groaned for poking her nose in his business, worried she might blab about the charge to his mother.

"He's hardly been out of sight since I arrived and hasn't been roaming while his bike is waiting for repair. I'm sure he didn't take it."

Joe owed her thanks once again for being a chaperone, to his great surprise.

The monk backed off. "Are you sure? Who else would take my bees' tonic?"

"You mean it's not honey wine?" Joe spluttered a laugh.

"It's certainly not alcoholic!" The monk looked like a teetotaller offended at being caught drunk. "It's a mix of vitamins and special oils that makes bees broody."

Joe revelled to think of his enemy guzzling a cocktail made to stimulate a queen bee's ovaries. Perhaps Brad would lay an egg! But, of course, Joe would face retribution for pulling a fast one if it made the bully puke.

Now in a more cheerful mood, the trio carried

protective clothing and tools a short distance from the shed to the monk's favourite hive. Emily looked horrified at the grime and wax on the spare bee suit but gamely pulled the leggings over her slacks and the zip under her chin. It looked like an astronaut's suit after she flipped the veil over her head and donned leather gloves.

He showed contempt for the session by pulling on his outfit back to front. Falling over a molehill served him right. Seeing impatience on the monk's face, Emily helped to tie the drawstrings and turn socks over the bottoms of his blue jeans. Joe felt like a trussed turkey in the butcher shop. The monk covered his own face with a veil draped from a sunhat but took no further precautions. Then, leaning an ear against the hive roof, he listened to thousands of tremulous wings and cracked a smile.

Emily crept forward to watch flights at the slit. "It's like a runway at Heathrow Airport without air traffic controllers," she said. When the covers came off, she stepped back to beside Joe. They expected an explosion of angry insects after disrupting placid lives. So it surprised them when the vast majority stayed at their stations on honeycomb frames hanging like folders in a filing cabinet. The monk puffed billows from his smoker to keep them hunkered down.

"Only a scaredy cat with binoculars would watch from that distance," he grumbled at them.

No teacher in Wimbledon would ever spoke that bluffly. But safe in her cocoon, Emily edged closer to look at the back of the hand the monk held out to show a crawling bee.

"See the pollen basket on her back legs? She brought it for house bees to feed to larvae."

"I thought they only drank nectar."

That opened a conversation between the two about insect diets. Joe felt snubbed for being ignored on a subject he knew about, so he tried to disrupt them with a cheeky question: "Please show us the king bee."

The monk rebuffed by turning his back on the boy. He leaned into the opened top to lever a frame with a steel tool. The bees had fused frames together with propolis resin which dries hard as bubble gum stuck under school desks by generations of boys. Then, muttering under his breath, he probed inside with a finger. Standing upright again, he shook his head. "Drat it!"

"Is something wrong, sir?"

"I thought I saw the Peacemaker queen, but she moved too fast to be sure. She shouldn't be away from the nursery."

"How can you know among so many workers?"

"I dabbed a yellow dot on her back. Let's see if she has laid eggs in the nursery box below."

The monk lugged four boxes off the tier to make a neat stack, leaving a pair on the base. After resting from the exertion, he separated several frames in the second storey nursery. By holding them up to the sun, he checked rows of cells for eggs the size of tiny rice grains.

"There she is, thank God, and laying an egg as I speak! How did she get down here so quickly?" He replaced the frames with the utmost care and inspected other boxes.

"Take it," he said, putting a frame in Emily's hands she held out to the limits of her reach. The order came too abruptly to refuse.

"Keep calm, Emily," Joe chuckled at her plight.

"You think you know about insects," she said without taking her eyes off the honeycomb. But I bet you've never been so close to this many bees or seen their babies."

It was true that Joe had only seen bee larvae in picture books. They were pale caterpillars, visible for a few days before disappearing under wax caps for the miraculous process that turned them into perfect adults. He wondered why metamorphosis happens in insects and frogs but not in humans. What would his mum do if she threw off the bed covers to see him lying on the mattress metamorphosed into a bug when he became a teenager? Run for a giant flyswatter!

Emily's arms sagged from the weight of the frame. It would shed insects if she rested it on the ground and would arouse the monk's temper. She felt as bound to the frame as if wearing handcuffs. Finally, she sighed when he returned it to a box and declared the inspection over. He had examined fifty frames in five boxes. Only later did they wonder if he didn't check the bottom box as an oversight.

"The hive may look chaotic inside, Emily, but it's a highly organised community," he said after removing his veil.

Joe hid a yawn inside his screen. *Oh no, he wants to give her a lecture!*

"Think of rows of cells like houses in your street, and each frame a different neighbourhood. Taken together, a hive is as complicated as your town with thousands of residents. You saw them scurrying to shops, factories and the airport. Some are builders and plasterers, some cleaners and janitors, some nurses and cooks, some security guards and a few royal courtiers. Many more commute to work in the fields and gardens. But here's the difference: they have the same mother."

They heard Emily giggling behind her screen. "The

workers all wore striped suits, and a few had big eyes like sunglasses. Are they the hive police?"

"Quite the opposite. They are lazy boys called drones."

Joe suspected the monk made a dig at him and sneered at her questions. *Will she never stop trying to be a teacher's pet?* He finally lost patience when she yammered about royal jelly in her mum's pantry.

"Tell her it's bee snot and see if she buys it again." He thought the Texan would approve of the wisecrack, even if insects don't have noses. Of course, the gag went down like a lead balloon.

"You aren't taking the lesson seriously, boy. Stop hiding your face behind the screen."

The sour face he concealed from them became serious when Emily violently shook her hand and exclaimed, "Ouch!"

"What's up, Emmy?"

She tore off a glove and shook it upside down. "What do you think, nitwit?" She scraped her wrist with a fingernail to remove a sting draped with the bee's guts. "I'm sorry you died for nothing."

Joe watched her nursing a welt. He checked if her lips turned blue or breathing became laboured, remembering his reaction to a wasp sting. Emily quickly calmed after the attack, but he still berated the monk for calling them gentle bees. He presented a corpse to the monk in his palm.

"Hmm. It has the same stripes as in the grumpy brood," Brother Adam told them, though they didn't understand what that meant.

After examining the swelling, Emily unfolded the tops of her cousin's socks. "Luckily, I tucked them over your trousers because you had a near miss. Did you feel them trying to get inside?"

The thought of bees crawling up his leg to investigate his private parts gave him profound anxiety and, of course, it didn't help to be reminded that he attracted them.

"Next time, tuck your trouser legs inside Wellington boots and get your mum to make a matching pair of fancy pants to go with your top." She meant it as sound advice, but Joe thought she wanted to dress him up as a drag queen.

They walked to the garden where Cuthbert beckoned from the bench. Brother Adam called from behind, "We are open to visitors for elevensies."

The younger monk had set four places on the table around a crusty loaf from his bakery. When he said grace, Joe nudged Emily to close her eyes, not a custom at her home. They slavered slices with butter and honey and filled glasses with apple juice.

"Help yourself to the pickings your friends left in the orchard," Cuthbert said, passing the jug to the boy. Emily didn't get the joke, but Joe knew what he meant.

Emily stifled a sneeze in her handkerchief. "My allergy is worse here than in London."

"There's tons of pollen in the next field," said Cuthbert, between chomping on a crust.

"Is it yellow mustard?"

"No, the farmer sells the crop for making vegetable oil," Adam scoffed. "No friend of our bees, he sprays the field with pesticides, yet they provide free pollination."

Emily blew her nose again. "I read that unfiltered local honey contains pollen grains that can cure a runny nose."

"Don't be daft, Emmy!" The boy's vehemence surprised them. "That pollen mostly stays inside flowers waiting for bees to collect it. Your hay fever is from breathing pollen blowing in the air from grasses and trees."

"The boy's got talent and is quite a naturalist." Cuthbert flashed him a smile and nodded to Emily. "Even if honey doesn't stop your sniffles, we can agree that it's scrumptious. My brother swears by it and never misses a day taking it for medication."

"So it's good for a monk's meditation too?" They all

laughed at Joe's bloomer, but Emily saw dimples in his cheeks that meant he was being sassy.

The chattier of the two monks, Cuthbert often spoke for his brother. He said the bee-yard was more than making honey and never intended to make money. It helped to preserve the abundance of nature. "Our hives and wild bees make a more bountiful landscape. When the bees are buzzing over my crops and flowers, I hear hymns of peace."

"They aren't always so gentle," Emily said, showing her wrist.

Cuthbert offered to get ointment from the infirmary, but she said it the sting had stopped throbbing.

"She's a trooper," Adam said. "But I despair of her cousin. He's like a timid conscript who doesn't want to leave the barracks."

The son of Oldburgh's hero hated the slur, especially in a girl's presence. Emily floated like a swan into the village, fêted by his mother and a model student to the monks. It was alright for her to feel as safe as in armour around hives while he stood half-clad.

Seeing the monk irritating her cousin, Emily asked why they called the queen in the solo hive the Peacemaker. Cuthbert seemed eager to explain.

"It began when I helped my brother on the moor—"

Adam cut him off and wagged his finger. "No! No! You force me to explain from the beginning.

"The old abbot wanted to restore the beekeeping tradition in the new monastery. We started from scratch after a disease wiped out native black bees in the country. The abbot sent me abroad to find robust yet well-mannered queens as founders of colonies. We named the stock after the village and their descendants exist in the grey hives and bee-yards around the globe. Some queens produced aggressive foragers that made pots of honey; others bred gentler bees loath to swarm. I wanted to create the perfect bee by cross-breeding the best characters in both."

Emily furrowed her brow at a lesson she remembered from school biology. Didn't the monk Gregor Mendel cross-breed pea plants from two varieties poles apart and never make a perfect blend? Crossing yellow and green peas, he only got yellows in the first generation. After that, he mostly found one type dominant from crosses of other characteristics.

"Sorry, I don't get it. Bees should be aggressive to keep thieves from stealing their honey."

Emily's argument got Joe thinking about the monk's experiment. Messing with nature by making unnatural crosses might create a Frankenbee, for wasn't that how scientists made killer bees?

Adam admitted that experts disagreed, but what did they know? He already managed a hundred hives when the professors were still in nappies. Besides, his favourite hive proved that bees can be gentle *and* productive. That's why he called them peacemakers.

He let Cuthbert take over the conversation, but the loner had proven he could break out of his shell, or as Emily joked privately— *out of his cell.*

"My brother kept the cross-bred hives on the heather moor," said Cuthbert. "They were safe from pests and pesticides in that remote place, even from an epidemic of mites he feared coming from the East. Each new generation improved on the previous one, and all went well until last summer—"

The brothers exchanged grim looks before Adam took up the story.

"We don't know if the blaze started from a lightning strike or someone carelessly dropping a cigarette. Call it an act of God or of man, but by the time we arrived, fire beaters had damped the flames and our hives had burnt to shells of charred wood and molten wax—all except one.

"The queen survived by a miracle. I brought her here to replace the resident queen in a grey hive, hoping the workers would accept her. Peacemaker settled in to make her own brood, which you saw flourishing today."

As the youngsters listened, the man grew more interesting in their estimation than his reputation as a wizened old crank. His drab robes covered a passion for giving something to the world. The bee-yard was a hermitage for perfecting bees away from prying eyes, and he kept guard from the shed.

But his project hung by a thread. He had only one queen until she produced daughters. Then, he could start new hives and breed even more peacemakers. When the news spread, beekeepers would come hammering on his door to buy perfect queens. As time ran out and weaker every year, he needed an extra pair of hands. And who did they belong to?

It made sense to have doves painted on the home of peacemaker bees, but something niggled Joe. He knew there must be more to the story from roaming the grounds for years.

"There was a painted hive before you moved it near the shed. Was that for another special queen?"

"He's got a sharp memory, brother," Cuthbert said. "There's been a painted hive in the lower meadow for as long as I can recall. You touched up the paint every year and said it was specially blessed, though I never knew why."

Brother Adam cleared his throat and turned to check the clock tower. "It's time for midday prayers," he said to close the meeting early and depart.

CHAPTER 6

Path to the Vampire Vault

Daisy plunged through a throng of bees to find Sundew sucking at a nectar booth with the guards. Shady gave her a frosty reception.

"You ought to be at work, Forty-Seven."

"Use my proper name instead of an insulting number." Daisy spoke more boldly in the absence of the police chief.

"Don't be insolent, you greasy weaxer," Shady snapped. "You have an unhealthy interest in this weirdo. Scram!"

She turned her back to ask the guards permission to walk with her friend. They didn't object as Captain Cornflower reluctantly allowed the insectors to employ them for escort duty.

"Daisy! I didn't expect to see you until tomorrow," Sundew exclaimed. "Why did you follow us?"

She came without a plan except to offer comfort and give a warning. "I believe Cockscomb is right. Bees aren't sent to the Cryptum as a competence test: they disappear inside."

"I know you mean well, Daisy, but your loathing of

insectors makes you blind. You know we must follow orders from elders because that's what it means to belong to a family. To be confined for a day is a small price for the rest of my life, and it won't be bad. I will still hear swusters humming in the box above and smell the cwen's perfume. If I run away, they will call me a coward and I won't be able to face anyone again."

"Don't throw your life away and make us grieve, Dewy. I can help you escape."

Daisy was willing to sacrifice a comfortable life by breaking the law, but Sundew refused to be treated like a newbie. "I'm old enough to make my own decisions now."

When the deputy heard the prisoner speaking, she barked at the squad to get moving again. Ordered to get lost, Daisy hung back wondering what to do, until a familiar voice called her name.

"So, there you are, Daisy." Hyacinth came up puffing after worrying her partner didn't turn up for work and asked around for the route taken by the escort. "I guessed you wouldn't give her up easily."

They hadn't gone far together when a baritone sing-song voice caught their attention. The guards couldn't budge Sundew from waiting for the other two to catch up for explaining the meaning of the lyrics. After a short discussion, they decided it was a nonsense verse.

> *Ich vittel puke dooma un bumba*
> *Mor joring con dirgit er sunda,*
> *Gird smish scratidly un Mangeapis*
> *Quy munchin hunig un bibis.*

The singer was larger than a worker bee but smaller than a queen or Sundew and wore a velvet fuzz around its middle. It had enormous eyes like a damselfly.

Shady bellowed at it, "Buzz off, you stupid bore, and don't interfere with official business."

Neither did Daisy have a kind word for the interloper. "He might go away if we don't encourage the scrounging broder," she muttered.

Until then, Sundew supposed she belonged to an exclusive matriarchy. She had met female field bees and female house bees and heard the queen addressed as a 'she'. So this creature was the first 'he' in her experience. An outcast herself, she found consolation from knowing that another kind of bee lived under the same roof with as much ridicule as she suffered.

"Do broders speak our language?" she asked a guard.

"They can when they feel like it. This one came droning gibberish about a mythical monster."

The other guard snickered, "There's nothing odder than

a broder. They loaf around sucking nectar they never gather and nibbling honey they don't make. Moreover, they can't qualify for sentry duty without a stenger. I will never understand why cwens tolerate the freeloaders."

The drone took the rejection in his stride, perhaps used to it. He seemed humbler than workers yet no less patriotic. "I am a son of the hyf as you are a daughter," he told Sundew, the only one willing to listen to him. "My great disappointment in life is to be named Deadnettle as if a broder can't be a patriotic hive defender."

When Sundew told him they were taking her to the Cryptum, he asked what crime she had committed.

"I'm not a common criminal," she replied, prickly. "They are putting me through a test before I join my team tomorrow."

Deadnettle still tagged along, unfazed after she snapped at him. "I'm heading there too. They detained Broder Bee Balm in the vault after a spy heard him celebrating an anniversary of Cwen Goldenrod's arrival."

Hyacinth urged them to shush to avoid getting into trouble. Angry at losing their queen, the police rounded up anyone who approved of the regime change.

They soon arrived at the bottom of the hive; the only box illuminated by an entrance slit. Comb-maidens waited on the ledge for food to be delivered while other house bees dumped waste over the side. None of them wanted to march into the darkness towards redundant combs that turned black and rancid in a hinterland of abandoned industry. They didn't encounter another soul on the next beat of the journey, not even a scavenging beetle or wax moth, until a bee crept out of the shadows to tap Daisy on the back.

"Don't be alarmed. I came to help your friend."

"Stop hassling us, whoever you are."

"Shush. I'm Cockscomb wearing pansy scent for disguise." The bee nervously eyed the deputy and guards. "I know how it feels to see someone you care about mistreated. The insectors took advantage of Sunnedew, but it's not too late to save her. We need stout fighters to rid the hyf of Hawbrods for restoring our peace."

"That's absurd. Revolutions build more resentment than lasting peace," Hyacinth hissed. "We need to show our opponents they have nothing to fear from our numbers and can live in a happy union. It's all about communication."

Daisy would have rolled her eyes if they weren't fixed in her head. She admired her partner's optimism but saw things differently, somewhere between the poles of appeasement and violent conflict.

"Our Modor rejects force except for our most implacable enemies," she said. "I don't want to be trampled on, but nor will I join your ragtag band. Today's rebels could become tomorrow's tyrants. I believe we must keep pushing for a fairer society and take knocks from insectors for protesting and disobedience if necessary."

Talk of moderation annoyed Cockscomb. She couldn't wait for a peaceful transition and blamed Goldenrod for being too soft by allowing Hawbrods to hold power over them. Hyacinth leaped to the defence. She said not all law-keepers were as toxic as Hemlock, and the new queen would fill vacant officer posts with their breed.

"You are complicit in an injustice if we fail to defend our swusters," Cockscomb harangued them. "Your friend is the latest victim, and you may be next."

"Perhaps we should try harder to persuade her to escape. I know a safe place at the top."

"Don't drag me into your schemes, Daisy. Nowhere is safe from spies."

Daisy sighed. Her partner always anticipated problems where she only saw opportunities.

Sundew edged closer, upset at being the subject of whispering. "Don't make plans behind my back. I won't slink off. Look at Deadnettle who puts you all to shame by obeying the duty to care for a broder."

Cheesed off for not winning the argument, Cockscomb sloped back into the shadows. And the partners felt snubbed by a friend they tried to advise. Their moods matched the cold, dank place as they trudged behind the squad.

To human ears, a 'Cryptum' sounds like the imposing basement of an abbey or a cathedral where effigies of bishops and nobles lie on marble slabs. The miniature version in the hive base was equally magnificent before bees overlaid it with a crust of propolis and turned it into a dungeon inhabited by mites.

As a witness to his brother's incarceration, Deadnettle knew where the jailors covered a hole with a blanket of beeswax. The guards chewed it open while others stood by to watch. He wanted to go inside first to search for his brother, but Shady forbade contact with the convict.

Meanwhile, Sundew's friends bickered about what to do as time ran out. Daisy wanted her partner to distract the guards while she slipped away with their friend. The idea horrified Hyacinth, who worried they would be condemned as felons for aiding an escape. She said they should leave fate to Sunne, although the sun's rays didn't penetrate the vault. The argument between partners became so intense they didn't notice the guards shoving Sundew into the black hole. She tried waving to get their attention before slithering out of sight.

Looking around and at the void, Daisy and Hyacinth realised she had gone, leaving them bitter and blaming each other for not saying farewell.

Hyacinth hastened back to her comb and Shady to other duties while Daisy stayed behind to mope. Finally, Daisy recalled an old refrain for troubled times that commended the care of a loved one to a mystical power: *May the shining Sunne defend and preserve you.*

CHAPTER 7
Test of Nerves

After the monks left the garden for the noon service in the abbey, Joe tossed the beekeeping outfit over his shoulder as a signal to Emily for them to go home.

"You like hobnobbing with the monks."

"What do you mean?" Emily looked hurt.

"You bombed them with questions all morning."

"I notice you don't mind their company when there's bread and honey for elevensies. Besides, you enjoy showing off your knowledge of insects."

"No, I don't!"

"If you like bugs so much, why are you nervous around the hive? Are you scared of getting stung or trying to drop out of lessons?"

Perhaps she misunderstood the arrangement, thinking he volunteered for free education during the holidays. If his mum hadn't explained to her, neither would he reveal the true reason for taking lessons in beekeeping or why bees made him nervous. They suspended the conversation because Emily couldn't take criticism from him, and he wouldn't admit if she was right.

At the gate, they stopped to gaze across the meadow. The grey hives gleamed in the sunshine, no longer hidden since Cuthbert scythed the long grass.

"He said a hundred hives, so where are the rest?" Emily asked.

"That was in prehistoric times when he was a young man but he only manages twenty hives now."

"I suppose you can tell how strong a colony is from the height of a hive." Emily began a circular tour of the group while he waited. She leaned over to check the activity at entrances and finally squatted at a tier of only two boxes.

"Don't get too close, Emmy. The Oldburgh bees aren't as friendly as in the solo hive. If you stir them up to sting me to death, I'll come back to haunt you."

Emily knew he spoke baloney after seeing him growing in confidence around hives and having seen little reaction from her sting. The worst that could happen to him would be if his mum sent him to the young nurse at the clinic who enjoyed jabbing boys with a steel stinger.

She returned looking scornful at Joe for not following her. "As a novice beekeeper, you shouldn't leave a guest to do your job. Go check the small hive. I'm sure it's dead and if it contains honeycomb you ought to save it before the ants find it."

She snatched the outfit off his shoulder. "You won't need this skimpy thing and will never have a safer opportunity for a first hive inspection on your own."

Joe hated to be goaded but didn't want to look like a sissy. So he walked to the back of the hive and peered down to ensure the entrance remained inactive.

"Go on! It's completely safe."

His heart throbbed as he lifted the covers, but she was right. The residents had died or deserted to leave frames bulging with honeycomb. He opened his knife to separate fused combs. Pulling out the first frame dripping with honey, he held it up in triumph like the big fish he hooked out of the river the last time he went with his dad.

She sat on his outfit and clapped hands. "You struck liquid gold and I bet there's more inside."

Honey continued to ooze out of damaged cells when Joe rested the frame against the hive body. A sample on his finger tasted as good as out of a jar. The neighbouring colonies had missed the opportunity to raid the county.

Emily watched as he pulled out more frames. "I think you have checked enough and should put them back," she said. "We'll call the monastery to let them know."

As he lowered the top cover, he noticed her gazing around with a hand covering her mouth.

"Don't stand there, Joe, you must run!"

Nothing he saw had changed, so he assumed she teased him. The bee-yard looked serene, although the other hives were too far apart to see activity at the entrances. He didn't notice that background humming had increased in volume. Hearing her call with greater urgency made him raise his gaze above the horizon. Swirling dots were more visible against a backdrop of white clouds. He marvelled at their antics as they zoomed around without bumping.

Although seeming at first to fly around aimlessly, they drifted in his direction and gradually descended to make him feel like the still eye of a dust devil as they circled. His first panicky impulse was to follow her order. They alighted on spilled honey to turn patches of grass beside him brown with their bodies. The first satiated bees zoomed away to dance in their hive for informing other foragers.

They were only interested in the sweet booty, but he quaked. Standing with a bare head and arms beside an air force of stinging insects he wouldn't have felt much more vulnerable if stark naked. The American beekeeper had warned they would go for his hair like a bull to a red flag, but the dread faded as Joe remembered the man liked to poke fun.

Emily continued shouting for him to retreat, but what did she know? A voice in his head advised him to stand like a totem pole with his mouth and eyes closed. So long and tightly did he screw up his face that he worried it would be set like a stone gargoyle on the abbey wall the next time he looked in a mirror. The interior voice exhorted him to hum, although it came out grating from nerves: *AUM— AUM—*

"Take the threat seriously, Joe, and stop pretending to be a Buddhist."

He wanted to tell Emily to shut up but didn't open his mouth because the smell of honey on his breath might attract bees. The worst of it was to feel his fingers tickled where he had held honeycomb. He resisted the temptation to wipe them on his trousers and regretted he hadn't dug his hands in his pockets before freezing.

When his eyes were shut, other senses became more acute and he felt more mentally alert, although imagining more bees on him than in fact. A few minutes seemed like hours until he cautiously looked through slitted eyes.

Most of the bees had left with full crops. Emily lay sprawled on his crumpled outfit as if sunning herself on the beach. She chuckled at getting him into a pickle. "I didn't hear you squawk, so I guess you are alright."

He bit his lip when he stole back to her, determined she wouldn't have the last laugh of the day.

They departed for home on a footpath through fields that traced the ancient parish boundary. Joe never saw the gang going that way. They halted at a spinney where countrymen used to coppice hazel branches to weave into fences. Neglect turned it into a wilderness where Joe liked to explore, and birders listened to nightingales after dark.

"You must keep it secret if I show you my camp."

He sprung ahead and through a wire fence to forge a path through dense undergrowth. Emily's cry made him smirk from picturing a barb catching her slacks. City girls were wimps who needed to learn the country craft.

"Don't ever bring me here again," she scolded him while negotiating a passage through a thicket of brambles. "I only agreed to see your stupid camp to please you after your ordeal. What's the quickest way out?"

"There's a shortcut through an electric fence."

Joe hid a grin as he led her to a clearing where he pointed to a treehouse made of planks on lofty boughs in an oak tree. She snubbed the offer to help her climb for a panoramic view at the top.

"I bet you aren't allowed to light fires here," she said, raking cold charcoal in a campfire ringed with stones.

He scuffed with his heel at objects glinting objects in the dirt. "I dropped my butterfly killing bottle here," he said and avoided her stare.

After leaving the woods, Emily hurried forward for a change of clothes in her aunt's cottage. On lifting the gate latch, she knocked a stub of red tubing off the post.

"Is this yours?"

She handed it over for him to roll in his fingers.

"Haven't you seen a dead shell from a shotgun before?"

He read the label silently: *Remington 12-gauge #9*. On the other side, he found a note scrawled in bold letters with a ballpoint pen: *A PRESENT FOR HOLY JOE*. He tossed it in the hedge before she saw it.

CHAPTER 8
The Troubles

After a lonely night in the bottom box, Daisy returned to the vault where the two guards stood on either side of the yawning hole. She poked a feeler inside to sniff.

"We couldn't stop your friend from going inside to look for his broder. He must be crackers," a guard told her.

She paced up and down, wheeling between irritation for them thinking she could befriend a drone and wondering why they kept the vault open. Did they expect Sundew to survive or wait for another prisoner? Perhaps the police were correct to accuse her of an unhealthy interest in the giant. The devotion of bees to their family doesn't extend to mutants regarded as foreigners.

She felt contrite for thinking even for a moment of ditching a friend. Besides, if they eliminated a half-queen, they might be emboldened to commit regicide. Of course, they should know that to murder a queen dooms a hive to extinction unless fertilised eggs exist to make a successor.

Queen Goldenrod's brood needed a champion with that rare combination of resilience and kindness to protect the monarch and her oppressed workers. Sundew was too raw for that role and lacked Hyacinth's skill in diplomacy, but who knew in the future? She had imposing looks and a stubborn belief in herself to her credit. Still, an illegitimate birth dragged her reputation down. Daisy suspected that onerous responsibilities elevate leaders to the company of eminent bees even in a society supposed to be equal. Better, therefore, for a dear friend to stay in a humble job rather than losing her through ambition, although a selfish wish.

The guards looked bemused as Daisy dithered about what to do. Few acts are as noble as saving the life of a friend, but would dying in the attempt foolishly throw her life away?

An impulse stirred her to stifle doubts. She squeezed through the hole into a darkness and silence as profound as in outer space. She needed to find Sundew's scent trail and leave her own to retrace her steps out.

Flakes covering the floor crunched under her feet and smelled of the remains of bees. They made her shudder. The Cryptum was a death cell, as Skunkie said. Breathing the dust of countless cuticles caused an explosive sneeze. The noise could alert friends and foes, so the return to silence felt disappointing and reassuring at the same time.

Beating wings to bounce echoes off the wall helped to navigate as the light contracted to a pinhole. When it winked out, she felt a pit in her stomach for being utterly alone and afraid the guards closed the hole.

A squeak confirmed she wasn't alone, but a scent doesn't travel fast in still air, so that couldn't send a signal from a distressed bee. Stopping to listen, Daisy heard the patter of tiny feet getting closer, going faster. They followed her trail, no longer concealing their intent as they raised high-pitched voices to warble a hunting song:

Free fry for fun,
I smell blood in a honeybee tum.
Be she alive or be she dead,
I'll suck her dry to make my bread.

Scrambling away, she stumbled over a desiccated cadaver that crumbled to dust. Trampling over it again moments later, she had run in a circle that gave flat-footed pursuers an advantage where they already knew every square inch of their home ground.

A low droning sound magnified her terror. Did the vampires have a gigantic mother mite? Dashing around in confusion, she eventually saw a friendly dot of light beckoning her back to the hole. She plunged through to land between the sniggering guards, never more pleased to see them.

Feelings of relief mingled with the disgrace of failing an

endeavour. She flopped down in despair. Nothing could move her except a pack of mites coming out of the vault. A sound averted all their eyes to the hole where a pair of feelers twitched. Daisy's heart leaped for a split second, hoping for her friend until two bulbous eyes turned her joy to annoyance.

"Deadnettle! You petrified me."

"I heard you sneeze and came out to say—"

"You ruined my rescue effort by scaring me out of my wits with your droning. Now, skedaddle. Vamoose!"

After he crawled away, Daisy pondered how to evade the mites. Perhaps they would ignore her next time if she masked her body odour or ate something unpalatable to them.

Feeling tired, she drifted into a nightmare that cast her back to when she was a helpless larva cradled in a cell. Eight-legged demons drummed on the lid and thrust needle-like tongues through the soft wax. Squirming in the confined space, she narrowly avoided getting sucked dry. A grating sound she assumed to be them lifting the cap woke her with a start but coming to her senses she realised the noise came from the hole. The guards fled as a head emerged, coughing hoarsely and too shrouded with dust to be identified. Still gathering her wits, she watched as it shook vigorously to uncover a golden body.

"Is that you, Daisy?" the insect croaked.

She struggled to speak, "Sunnedew! This is your second birth." The pair spread their feelers for a tight embrace and danced around.

"Sorry, I was stupid to trust the insectors and not listen to you. They knew I couldn't defend myself from a tiny enemy in the vault. I wish I took your advice to escape earlier but now we can get away."

"The guards scrammed when you gave them the willies coming out like a ghost. Let me groom you to avoid frightening our friends away before we leave."

"Please mind the tender place on my back where a blodsouker bit me."

"What happened?"

"Soon after I went inside, I met a bee almost drained of blood and so shrivelled I mistook her for Bee Balm. They cruelly imprisoned her for ridiculing an insector. She told me the floor was littered with the cuticles of bees and I would soon join them. Unfortunately, I arrived too late to save her and almost suffered the same fate.

"When a mite jumped on my back, I couldn't shake it off and heard it gurgling contentment from drinking my blood. Squeezing my scent in alarm automatically, I didn't expect anyone to notice. I thought I must be the only live bee left in the Cryptum, but then he came along—"

"You mean Deadnettle?"

"With his little jaws, he reached under the shell to gnaw the devil's feet until it clung only by its tongue and could be punched off. We ran to avoid a counterattack but got separated in the dark. I hope they didn't get him."

"He came out already."

"We promised to wait here for each other."

"I'm sorry for shooing him off," Daisy said. "Droning on about nonsense annoys me, but I feel awful now and will try to be kinder to broders in future."

"I also learned a harsh lesson today. The world isn't as kind as I thought, and I swear to get even with the Hawbrods."

"The Cwen forbids us from taking revenge."

"I can't forgive them even if she can."

Daisy felt sorry for her friend's loss of innocence and harder heart. She knew that not all Hawbrods were cruel and that some mites preferred a vegetable diet to sucking insect blood. The world wasn't black and white, but she had no time to convince Sundew when they heard footsteps.

"It's too late for a getaway. The guards are back with you-know-who, so try to look indomitable," Daisy urged her as the police chief marched up flanked by guards.

Hemlock gritted her jaws before swearing at them. "Holy frass! We have a special penalty for anyone breaking the rules of our test and another for those who aid them."

"You are a pitiless, horrid liar," Sundew said, stepping in front of Daisy to challenge the chief with the ugliest adjectives she knew. "You will receive justice for your deeds one day."

Hemlock hesitated to press charges against a giant and and had never been challenged like that before. A slippery character, she changed her attitude to avoid a setback to her authority. Drawing closer so Daisy didn't hear, she whispered, "You are too smart to be wasted on dullards. I can offer you a comfortable living as a lieutenant in my unit for overseeing others—"

"You tempt me to betray my friends? You deserve to sizzle in the noirbitel's firebox!"

They were still glaring at each other when Shady arrived with a pair of gummers nudging a young worker forward. Their attention was diverted by mocking voices behind:

> *Now that Hawthorn's dead*
> *We love Goldenrod instead.*
> *Hemlock doesn't care about tuppence*
> *But she will get a comeuppance.*

Sundew would have giggled at Cockscomb striding ahead of her cronies if the prisoner dragging her feet didn't look so forlorn. The gummers were hired to seal Sundew and the prisoner in the Cryptum. She wanted to box Hemlock on the head but knew it is nobler to save a life than take one. She charged at Shady, instead, bowling her over and urged the prisoner to run with her to the wall. The mob cheered the fugitives while Hemlock cursed her floundering deputy.

The fugitives paused in the storey above to exchange names and personal details. The insectors had condemned the prisoner, Bramble, for taking an unauthorized flight as an impulsive youngster. Quickly bonding from hatred of a common enemy, the pair mingled with their own brood. They thought they were safe until a noisy disturbance gave them qualms. But instead of a search party, a bee speckled with red pollen surged through the crowd.

"Too many spies here," Cockscomb whispered. "After your glorious escape, you need a haven until we can break the yoke of the Insectorate."

"We can look after ourselves."

"Don't be louse-headed, Sunnedew. You must lie low until they stop looking for you. Go to the empty quarter in the top box where you won't be disturbed except by the noirbitel."

Sundew remembered how its claw tried to grab her, although she was more worried if a posse found them. The renegade told them to wait until she returned and would send Deadnettle with food. No one would suspect a drone of collaborating with rebels.

The days dragged without work, so the runaways exchanged life stories that bolstered a mutual loathing of the other brood. So when Cockscomb reappeared, she found them eager to join her new army.

She led them to a secret location in a nursery annexe where hundreds of partisans had gathered. She wanted Sundew to give a testimony about her persecution, hoping it would kindle the smouldering revolution.

Hyacinth listened in astonishment through an adjoining wall as Sundew mounted the podium, although too shy to say much. Cockscomb took her place to stir the crowd's fervour with a silver tongue. She described how the giant bee had broken out of the death cell and foiled the custody of another innocent bee. Besides those facts, she shamelessly invented exploits that Sundew knew to be untrue.

In trepidation, Hyacinth squeezed into the rally to watch her friend showered with accolades. Sundew enjoyed the veneration as the War Council's figurehead. It went to the head of the young celebrity fawned over by mature bees who gave her delicious food in tribute.

Eventually, Hyacinth crept close enough to give advice, "You may find fame isn't the bliss you assumed." But her friend listened more closely to Cockscomb announcing a tour of the hive. Sundew bubbled with excitement at the chance to see industries she expected to join in future. The renegade leader sneered at the small ambition, saying routine jobs were okay for dummies, but exceptional bees deserved better. When Sundew didn't demur, Hyacinth crawled away with a broken heart.

Council members snaked after the leader to view occupations ranging from nursing to housekeeping to honey-cooking. The grand spectacle of a revolving wheel of hive life left them in awe and proud to see workers serving the common good without complaint. But Cockscomb hadn't brought them on a sightseeing tour. She came to recruit troops despite elders protesting that transferring prime workers would weaken the engines of industry.

After an exciting day, Sundew snuggled down for the night among comrades, although her mind still buzzed.

What did Cockscomb expect her to do? Was there still time to make peace with the Hawbrods? What was the price of waging war? While turning these thoughts over, news rippled across the sleeping quarters to rouse everyone for chattering to neighbours.

"Hard to believe it could happen again—"

"Just when she thought it was safe—"

"She's done for this time—"

"What's going on?" Sundew wiped a bleary eye, wondering if they talked about her.

"The enemy arrested Bramble."

"It can't be true. She lay down beside me."

"Cockscomb gave her a message last night to take to allies hiding in Box 3."

"Why would she send gentle Bramble to a risky place?" Sundew asked, but the informer only gave a knowing look.

The seeds of violence watered by Cockscomb now germinated and flourished. It only took the sacrifice of one innocent bee—one more drop of resentment—to trigger a civil war between broods.

Although still dark outside, the bees trooped to an assembly point where they lined up and rattled their stings. Cockscomb stood on the back of a recruit as a platform for calling them to attention.

"We have endured persecution while the Hawbrods reserved the best jobs and food for themselves. Denied justice without an impartial jury, our swusters have received harsh punishments for minor crimes. Remember those who vanished without a trace. If Sunnedew hadn't come out of the Cryptum alive we would still be in the dark about where the Disappeared went. And now Bramble is sent there too.

"If they call us friends, do you trust them? When they pledge loyalty to our Modor, do you believe them? I heard them saying the old cwen will return, or a young pretender will replace Goldenrod. These are treasonous plots.

"But without a cwen to lay eggs, their workers become older and frailer. In desperation, they will try anything to dominate us, and attempted to kill Sunnedew, the cream of our brod."

Delighted to have a new champion, voices in the assembly begged to give Sundew a royal title and chanted: *Hail the Sunne Cwen.* She lowered her head, fearful of challenging the throne. Cockscomb restored order by declaring their forces would turn a page of history that day to build a new society. She told them to prepare for resistance because revolutionary changes never happen without disruption and sacrifice.

"I implore you to join our army. Recruiting officers are standing by for loyal volunteers to sign-up."

Hundreds of bees from Goldenrod's brood surged forward into queues. Cockscomb swaggered along the lines, picking the sturdiest individuals as captains of companies and lieutenants for platoons. She divided the troops into three brigades, calling them Liberty, Agility and Purity. Volunteers were turned away if they didn't have matching stripes. Hawbrods switching to their side were suspected as secret enemy agents, and drones who professed to be fighters were rejected for being unarmed and having pacifist sympathies.

Cockscomb divided the army into campaigns inside and outside the hive. She ordered Sundew to stay behind the front lines for giving field commanders tactical advice from intelligence reports of spotter flights scouring the battlefields.

It was frustrating to miss the action. Hearing the electric roar of wings outside, she couldn't resist the temptation to peer out of the entrance. The air was filled with the chaos of clashing legs and jaws that forced opponents to crash with broken wings. It reeked of a banana smell squirted by fighters in the stress of combat. Ground forces also fought ferociously and showed no mercy to captives.

A clap of thunder announcing a summer squall prevented greater loss of lives. Forces outside scurried to shelter in the hive to avoid getting wet and the rising humidity inside damped the fighting spirits of the rest. A double rainbow stretched across the heavens after the rain clouds retreated.

Standing at the entrance, Sundew asked returning fighters for news. Among hundreds of casualties, she heard of two waxers on her team who had been slain. Among reports of fatalities inside, Bramble died in a fray from partisans wrestling with Hawbrods escorting her to the vault. Hemlock had gone into hiding.

Wounded bees limping back wouldn't live long enough to become honoured veterans. The injured legs and wings of insects cannot heal, and physical handicaps are liabilities in a work-obsessed community. The lives of bees are as tragic as they are marvellous.

The war officially ended with a truce, although the Goldenrod brood crowed that they triumphed. They cancelled a victory parade to avoid stirring more enmity. Other celebrations fizzled out after weighing the double penalty of a violent war. The bees grieved for partners and lamented the damage to honeycomb. They had heavier workloads now and fewer guards to defend the home.

Hence, the victors asked the vanquished to help restore the hive. At first, they gave each other shifty glances, but mutual interests soon sealed a cooperation.

Meanwhile, Sundew fretted about a battle that failed its mission to rid the hive of those tormenting her brood. Her side had gained nothing, and she needed a new role after the army disbanded. After being gloried as the brood's darling, workers now scurried past to avoid conversation with a former warmonger. She didn't care for public opinion as much as Daisy's eyes that strenuously avoided hers. Only one bee stared back, a ragged individual with white bristles.

"Hey, who do you think you're looking at?" Sundew challenged her.

A courier running up bowed at the old bee before giving an army report. The deference affronted the dignity that Sundew had enjoyed in wartime.

"Let me see the report," she insisted.

"Don't you know who this is?" the messenger snorted. "Who do you think you are to deserve privileged information? As our storyteller, Sage is the first to receive information for broadcasting hyf news."

Sundew recalled hearing the name before and that hive history was carefully preserved but hadn't connected the two. Other workers evidently knew because they gathered around Sage as the messenger read names aloud to her.

"We have lost "Lavender[57], Petunia[401], Bramble[15], Cherry[98] and Zinnia[25] . . ." The list went on for several minutes before she mentioned others missing in action, including General Cockscomb and two captains. Finally, Sage asked for the names of fallen Hawbrod fighters so they would not be ignored.

"Dear-oh-dear," the ancient bee mumbled. "The Cwen will be heartbroken by the waste of lives. How many more are wounded?"

"We are still compiling that list, Madam, but I recall Lavender[231], Salvia[69], Hyacinth[135]—"

Daisy cried out from the back of the crowd, "Wait! Did you say Hyacinth? Is she badly hurt?"

The news gutted Sundew, but her friend's stern look before dashing away discouraged her from following. She lashed out at Sage instead. "You can look smug since you have a new story to tell, but the rest of us are losers."

"Aren't you ashamed for breaking the Beeattitudes?"

"The Bee-what . . .?"

Sage looked exasperated. "I want you to attend the special assembly I am calling for later."

CHAPTER 9
The Oldburgh Mystery

Emily had no time to kick her heels between helping in the shop and the bee-yard. She yearned for a free day to hang out in the village. At the first opportunity, she dawdled outside shop windows while Joe trotted ahead to meet the monk.

"Go ahead, and I will catch up with you later," she said.

"I'm making my own hive today," Joe called back. "He promised me a 'nuc' to start my own colony next year."

She wasn't astonished by the sudden enthusiasm because they both went full-on with new projects. She had a passion for writing stories, and he had an absorbing interest in insects. Making pocket money from honey was an extra incentive. Joe disappeared through the monastery gate while she knocked on her aunt's shop door ahead of opening time.

"Hello, dear. I thought you planned to explore the village today."

"I'm stumped for ideas what to give Dad for his birthday." She hoped her dad's sister had ideas after a fruitless search that morning.

"He might like a jar of our honey," her aunt replied.

Still unsure, Emily wandered up and down the aisles, perusing the merchandise. Returning empty handed to the counter, she flipped through a brochure.

"I didn't know you had an earlier abbey. Reminds me of a history class about the Dissolution of the Monasteries."

Her aunt told her a majestic abbey once stood on the same grounds. After King Henry's commissioners shut it down, villagers carted stone and slate away to build a parish church and their own homes, including the cottage where she lived. Nothing remained above ground of the medieval building that had attracted pilgrims to venerate the reliquaries of saints in the abbey treasury.

"After the Great War, Abbot Wilfrid planned a new monastery and hired local workmen to build on the old foundations. Be careful of uneven ground where people dug trenches searching for an antique box."

"What kind of box?" It didn't take much to rouse Emily's curiosity.

"Before my time," her aunt smiled. "The abbey became wealthy from people making gifts in exchange for the monks' prayers. It's said they hid a treasure box to avoid confiscation by the royal commissioners."

"That's as fascinating as Captain Kidd's pirate treasure."

"The last monk carried the secret to his grave. It faded

into a legend until a century ago when builders stumbled on a clue while refurbishing the manor house on Farthing Lane. They found a tiny chamber under the floorboards containing a bed, candlestick, and potty. The last resident left a parchment scroll and rosary behind a wall panel. Have you heard of a priest hole?"

"Catholics hid priests in their homes in times of persecution. Does the scroll have anything to do with the box?"

"Absolutely everything," her aunt cried. "Perhaps a monk gave it to a priest going into hiding. It shows a map marked with an X where they buried it on the grounds. You can see it exhibited at the Windcomb museum. Imagine villagers racing to the ruins with picks and spades when the news got out. No rules or officials existed to stop them in the eighteen-eighties. I expect they worked harder that day than they ever did on farms and gardens but found nothing."

"What a pity to never know."

Perhaps her aunt was sorry to spoil a natural curiosity because she brought the story up to date after a moment's hesitation.

"The box was forgotten until Wilfrid started building a new abbey forty years later. One of the workmen struck an object with his spade where treasure hunters hadn't looked under the former chancel. He thought it was only a lump of flint but unearthed a box."

"Wow! It gets more exciting!"

"Hmm. I wish it stayed in the ground because it created a heap of trouble."

She crossed the aisle to adjust jars lined up in already neat rows. It was a sign she didn't want to say more, perhaps worried the girl would press her with more questions. Emily wouldn't let the subject drop and resented the evasion, feeling almost adult at age sixteen.

"I suppose the workman couldn't keep it. There's a law to hand over a treasure trove to the government. Or I suppose the Vatican in Rome owns it if it's discovered on church property."

"I can't say, dear. The abbot took it away, and we never heard anymore."

The ringing doorbell announcing a customer halted the conversation. Emily picked up the brochure again until her aunt was free.

"I'm surprised it doesn't mention Brother Adam on this page about the abbey's hives." She felt sorry if a lifetime of service had been overlooked.

"There's an older history. You can see the original

beekeeper pictured in an abbey window."

Emily slipped out when a lad arrived with a basket of loaves from the monastery bakers.

With nothing better to do, Emily strolled to the abbey. Church buildings were unfamiliar to her family, who only attended them for weddings and at Christmas, and then only maybe. She hurried across the courtyard to beat a busload of tourists inside.

Wandering between the pews, she gazed at the vaulted ceiling and across the nave at prophets and saints in stained-glass windows. The sound of footsteps behind turned her head to a young man in a cassock and dog collar.

"Welcome to the abbey, miss. We have booklets about Saint Benedict for only fifty pence," said he.

"I came to see a picture of an ancient beekeeper."

The priest pointed to the east transept where the sun shone through a window. It brilliantly illuminated a black-robed man with a halo crowning his tonsure. One of his hands touched a wicker skep, a primitive type of beehive made from woven straw. The other curled around an arrow stuck in his chest, yet he had an angelic smile. Helmeted men rowed a square-rigged longship in the blue background. Emily skipped back to ask the priest.

"It's a memorial to Abbot Wilfrid, for restoring beekeeping to the abbey. Our shop sells honey and mead from Brother Adam's bees."

"Oh, you mean the abbot who found the Oldburgh treasure!" She connected with the story told by her aunt. "Do you know about it?"

"Nothing, I'm afraid, but I pray it's in safe hands."

That sounded like more evasion, but Emily took it as a sign the horde still existed. She hurried out to the garden bench where they had elevensies with the monks, her head mushrooming with ideas for a story based on an exciting blend of beehives and treasure, kings and Vikings. Only chirping sparrows broke the peace she needed for thinking.

Stumbling over a juicy mystery didn't happen every day. The cagey behaviour of adults could mean the box had never left the grounds. Perhaps a sly old abbot habituated to tradition hid it again to honour the intentions of his ancient predecessors.

Puzzling over the monks' hiding place drove her mind down rabbit holes. The spot had to be craftier than under floorboards or in a bare cell that monks call a bedroom. They might not have access to a safe. She feared if it was lost forever from reburying in the holy dirt under tons of stone in the new building. But by drawing a map, the monk intended it wouldn't be lost forever, and his successors might feel the same. She considered the options for reburial on the monastery's extensive grounds and how the spot could be flagged more reliably than on a scrap of parchment.

Her eyes drifted in a wide arc to the path leading to the shed via the orchard and graveyard. Images of gravestones triggered a brainwave. What safer place than on consecrated grounds where only gravediggers disturb the lawn? A dummy headstone might mark the spot only known to the brethren. After giggling at her ingenuity, Emily sighed as she hauled back a wild imagination more worthy of a novel.

Nevertheless, she loitered in the graveyard to read the names of deceased monks on marble headstones and crosses and then visited a whitewashed building on a low mound. A pair of carved cherubic faces stared out of the limestone wall on either side of a door shaped like a bishop's mitre. Emily tried to shove the unlocked iron bolt but couldn't budge it to look inside.

Brother Cuthbert startled her when he heard the door rattle but didn't ask about the disturbance to avoid embarrassment. She sat on a bench while he remained standing beside his scythe with the crescent blade resting on the ground.

"What's the little building for?" she asked. "It would make a fine chapel for hobbits."

The monk bent over, laughing. "It's a mausoleum if you know what I mean?"

"That's a tomb for an important person."

"Exactly. It's the tomb of Abbot Wilfrid, who died when I was a young monk."

Emily imagined the old abbot blessing the brethren and passing secrets to them on his deathbed. Perhaps he entrusted one with the box, which was fast becoming an obsession.

It would be widely known if the valuables had been sold at auction or donated to a museum. A lack of information implied they never left the monastery, possibly still hidden in a nook close by to keep an eye on them. The mausoleum filled her gaze with new significance. Monks had access to it, but treasure hunters wouldn't think of looking inside. She burst to ask Cuthbert but dared not arouse his suspicion. To show immense curiosity could make him withdraw like a tortoise into its shell, so she chose words carefully.

"What's it like in the mausoleum?"

"It's empty apart from a stone slab. No heap of bones like a Roman ossuary." He laughed again. "My brother sweeps and checks the mousetrap, but Brother Baldred can't come since he moved to a nursing home."

Earnest questions about his community made him chattier. He told her that Adam came as a teenager after losing his father at the same age as Joe. The abbot named new postulants alphabetically in order of arrival. A for Adam, B for Baldred, C for Cuthbert, et cetera. They sounded more religious than baptismal names. Cuthbert said it would never do to call a monk Brother Baldrick because there was no saint with that name.

She thought the abbot would likely trust the three original brothers more than the scholarly monks who joined later. As the first, Adam was the most likely keeper of the mystery.

"I like Brother Adam, but he's not as I imagined a monk."

"Am I a closer fit?" Cuthbert patted his paunch and grinned.

Emily wondered how he kept his spirits up like a jovial

uncle. Weren't the monks' lives endless cycles of work and worship without the pleasure of possessions in a comfy home?

"Do you mind if I ask if your life gets boring?" The question could offend a pricklier monk.

"Not at all. I play the Grim Reaper, keeping company with sleepers under this lawn." He waggled the scythe. "The beekeeper spends most of the day with insect friends. People do him an injustice by mocking him for talking to bees. In the olden days, family news was often shared with the residents of backyard hives before telling neighbours."

"You, too, have a connection with nature."

"And I saw you having a peaceful time in the garden. You don't have that in London, though I've never been there. Have you considered if this life would suit you?"

The thought of entering a nunnery made Emily laugh, but only to herself to avoid hurting his feelings.

"What else can you do after leaving school?"

"I love to make up stories and want to be a writer."

"Where do your ideas come from?"

"Out of the blue or from experience. I'm sure there's a story here about the partnership between bees and monks. They make honey: you sell it. They build cells to make honeycomb: you live in monastery cells. They are celibate workers with a queen bee: you have a king monk of sorts if you pardon my meaning."

Brother Cuthbert looked askance, unsure how to reply to wild opinions. So she switched the subject to ask about the abbey window.

"You mean the martyr Eadwig who sounds like a bug? Ha, ha! My brother organized a campaign to pay for the window honouring Abbot Wilfrid who appointed him as our beekeeper all those years ago. If he had the pope's ear, I'm sure he'd beg to make Eadwig the patron saint of beekeepers."

"I've heard others speak reverently about that abbot. Didn't he find an old box from excavating the ruined abbey?"

"I only heard about it, Emily."

"My aunt said Joe's grandad had something to do with it."

Cuthbert bit his tongue. She worried if he had clammed up, but it was only a pause to decide it did no harm to share general knowledge.

"I don't know more than Mrs B. She probably told you Norma Grattich left our refectory staff to be a care assistant in the nursing home. We think her new husband insisted because there's bad blood between his family and us."

"I know Mr. Grattich is the father of the gang leader."

"The problem started with the boy's grandfather, who found an old box while excavating the abbey's foundations. The foreman took it away for Wilfrid to look after. That was Joe's grandad, and the Brawson and Grattich families haven't got along ever since."

"What did the abbot do with it?"

"As a holy man, I'm sure he did the right thing. However, Mr. Grattich senior kept pressing a claim for a reward and accused the abbot of hiding it. Let's talk about something more positive, like the huge change in your cousin."

"He's loath to admit a serious interest in bees. But he no longer dilly-dallies before meeting your brother and is making his own hive as we speak."

"Sounds like a parable of a penitent scrumper," Cuthbert chuckled, but she wondered what he meant. "My brother never wanted to have a helper, but he needs one now. He's desperate to secure his prize brood before retiring and must convince Abbot Godwin not to sell the hives to a firm. Bees don't have a place in his plan for expanding a spiritual retreat where insects could bother guests. Imagine my garden without bees or my brother without beehives. He's never closer to God than beside them. They are his gift to the world, and I fear closing the yard will kill him."

"I hope Joe can help after the holidays." Emily checked her wristwatch and stood to leave.

"I have a story about him if you can wait."

She sat down again, unsure if she wanted to hear about Joe's latest mischief.

"Promise not to think me a superstitious black monk," Cuthbert said, suddenly becoming solemn. "It's hard for outsiders to comprehend our community, which is nothing like a hive. We may look alike in our robes and have similar beliefs, but that's all. My high-brow and mystical brothers have spiritual rewards, but what rapture can a gardener expect—dreams of bountiful vegetables?" She kept a straight face. "I want to tell you something that happened after collecting tools from the shed this morning. I saw your cousin at the hive."

"He's helping with inspections now."

"That's surprising enough after his terror of getting stung, but he didn't wear any protective gear. I had to pinch myself to check I was awake when he lifted frames with bare hands to commune with insects. I crept away without letting him know I was there to avoid spoiling a transcendental moment."

Emily had noticed Joe's new boldness, although this brazenness surprised her. The scene moved Cuthbert in ways she could never feel because Joe was her cousin and a boy who could act rashly.

"I've seen him scatter-brained," she said, thinking of him humming beside a grey hive in a cloud of bees. "One day, he'll be a cropper for thinking they won't sting."

On her way to the shed, she felt sorry for pouring cold water over a vision that made the day special for Cuthbert. She mused if he perceived something profound to which she was blind.

Joe sat on the shed threshold, humming to himself while the monk sawed a wooden board on the bench. Everything looked normal.

"Hi, Joe. Did you check the hive today?"

Joe wondered how Emily knew but didn't look up. He waited for glue to set on the sides of a frame.

"Did you inspect it?" she repeated with a raised voice.

He blew aside a plug of beeswax to speak. "I found lots of dead bees there."

"That's shocking news. What happened to them?"

"Bees are always around the shed, attracted by the smell of honeycomb, but it stayed quiet all morning except for one pesky bee. It followed me everywhere, so I walked it back to the hive, where I found a heap of bees. I opened it to check the rest were okay."

He never expressed regret for killing butterflies, perhaps as a fair game like fish in the river. It had taken close observation of the home lives of bees to regard them as cherished individuals.

"I told the monk a raiding party probably came from the grey hives. We would have lost more bees if the rain hadn't stopped them from fighting. But instead of thanking me, the old stick said I'm getting too big for my boots." The racket in the shed prevented the monk from hearing.

"Don't be bitter. You know what the brood means to him."

When the noise ceased, Emily greeted the monk, "Good morning, sir. I'm sorry to hear about the bees."

"A grievous loss, but it's still a strong colony. So this is your last visit to my yard. I will miss you, Emily, and the boy, too, when he goes back to school." Joe made an ugly face for taking second place.

"The residents of your hives will also miss the bee whisperer," she chipped in. "Perhaps he will befriend other insects."

"Not wasps," Joe hissed. "I would like to make killer

bees pets for setting on Brad like rottweilers on six legs."

A casual remark not intended to be taken seriously provoked a reaction from the monk. "What's the matter with you? One minute you pour pity on bees, and the next, you want to hurt another boy. I thought working with the Peacemaker brood would rub off a kindly spirit. Don't forget the lion that lay down with the lamb."

After the monk left, Joe whispered to Emily with a sheepish grin, "The lamb was missing when the lion got up."

The girl gave him a puzzled look, never having attended Sunday school to read the biblical verse. Nevertheless, he knew the monk meant in an ideal world and wasn't such a fool to think a predator could become a vegetarian.

Emily agreed to go home via the boundary path if they avoided the spinney. It gave her more time to share what she had learned about the abbot's treasure. She pressed Joe for information, but he resisted, more interested in spotting birds and butterflies. Finally, he told her his dad thought it was a silly myth, knowing that would stop her yammering.

"You should be more curious because it's your village history. If they made it up, people wouldn't be so button-lipped, and I bet the monk knows more than anyone. Of course, we can't ask him." She dropped the subject in frustration.

A screech of brakes behind made them jump off the path in opposite directions as a teenager brushed between them, leaning low over the handlebars.

"An ape could ride better than you!" she yelled at the receding cyclist who looked back with a broad grin. "Did you see his black eye, Joe?"

"I expect old man Grattich bashed him."

"You thought we were safe going this way, but perhaps the gang is spying on us."

CHAPTER 10
Sage Lessons

The hive returned to tranquillity after the air cleared of the taint of war. House bees headed back to their combs. Foragers departed for the garden. Guards familiar with the small keeper didn't hassle him when he came to open the hive.

The two broods set aside grievances for the urgent work of feeding larvae and repairing damaged cells. Sundew still drifted around after the embarrassing meeting with Sage, but everyone was too busy to pay her attention. The time for flattery was over, and now unemployed, she had less status than the workers who used to bow to her.

After moseying around, she noticed bees leaving their stations to stream towards the wall. Without knowing what firm purpose drove them, she drifted with the flow to avoid getting in their way.

"Why the haste?" she asked one of them.

"Didn't you hear Sage calling us to a special assembly to review recent events?"

She had pushed it to the back of her mind because a public gathering risked exposing her to disgrace for involvement in the recent Troubles.

The traffic stopped in an empty frame the bees used as an auditorium. Most rows had already filled, so she entered one at the back, hoping to be unnoticed. On hearing her name mentioned by bees in another row, she felt the urge to dash to the exit, but too late. The ends of her row were occupied, and no one wanted to move for the giant to squeeze past when Forget-Me-Not climbed on stage.

The announcer called for patience while the storyteller finished a meeting with the queen. Sundew wondered why they gave a retired commoner so much respect. The sound of shuffling further down the row turned heads as Daisy apologised for letting her through with Hyacinth limping. So her friends hadn't ditched her.

"I'm very glad to see you," Sundew cried with delight. The pair approached in silence until Hyacinth replied to her question about the wounded leg.

"I broke my knee when they tried to press-gang me into the army. The handicap kept me out of the war, but I'm now disqualified from some jobs for life."

"You know what that means, Dewy?" Daisy said. "She can't be an effective forager without both back legs for carrying pollen. I will remain a house bee if she needs help at work, so they won't treat her like trash."

The two sisters were devoted to each other despite their differences and arguments, which Sundew found moving. They were hissed to keep quiet out of respect for the storyteller arriving on stage.

Hyacinth lowered her voice to a whisper. "If Sage tells us myths, don't think of them as old yarns. They explain who we are, where we come from, and what we can be. Stories unite us to make a happier and more productive family—"

She broke off as Sage began a speech.

"Dear swusters, our ancestors in the Dawning Times nested in hollow trees vulnerable to attack by robbers. So they made a treaty with bitels that walk on two legs, giving them hunig for rent in exchange for a straw hyf. But, unfortunately, the arrangement worked better for them than for us. Our new keepers had to destroy our homes to reap their harvest every summer, forcing families to rebuild bare hyfs for repeating the tragic cycle."

The audience turned to their neighbours in shock. Until recently, they lived in golden times and assumed every generation before had been entitled to a prosperous and serene life in a secure home.

After pausing to let the information sink in, Sage continued, "The history of progress is the unfolding of great events and the acts of generous and ingenious individuals. We took a giant step forward by changing straw hives to permanent habitations made of wood, and in the olden days when we were still ruled by kings, we also had a social revolution."

This disclosure made the audience gape. A small bee on the front row spoke for all when she asked, "You mean we were ruled by a faeder and a modor?" Hyacinth murmured the questioner was Rose, the hive poet.

"It is indeed true," Sage replied. "The last faeder of a dynasty was a dictator, and woe betided anyone opposing him, even the cwen. He lived extravagantly in a royal suite, waited on by swusters and entertained by dancers and hummers. He only left his chamber to hunt bugs and indulge other blood sports with the broders. They brought home fresh game and carrion for feasting in a great hall like this one, storing the surplus until it rotted to become tender and tasty. The broders swigged vintage nectar throughout the meal and sang:

> *Fill the pot, Fill the pot,*
> *Let it rot, Let it rot,*
> *Make it pour, Make it pour,*
> *Gimme more, Gimme more—*

"The swusters served meat for the main course and rare

honey for dessert. They grumbled about the exploitation while preparing their vegetarian meals. Besides cooking, cleaning and serving food, they had to contend with scavenging waesps and bitels. Only the broders owned stengers, but they were too lazy to chase them away.

Sage paused again to let them absorb another scandal. No one imagined female bees were servants or powerless to defend the hive.

"A beastly foe smelling food," Sage resumed, "came prowling at dusk when the king and broders were occupied with sports contests after dinner. They called it the Mangeapis."

The name sparked an outburst of hissing from remembering a monster thought only to exist in cradle lullabies. Someone raised a feeler to ask, "Why didn't they drive it off?"

"Unfortunately, the king gave a lousy example to numbskull broders distracted by sports and high living. We might still be under that yoke if the cwen hadn't devised a cunning plan that changed bee history.

"She presented the king with an ultimatum one day when the guards reported a musky odour forewarning of an attack. The broders had to lay down their weapons before the games started, or she would cancel the meal service to save contestants from getting injured by accidental jabs. Snorting at her audacity, the king gave in and told the broders it was his idea.

"Then the queen gave secret instructions to her swusters to fill cells around the hall with fermented honey from a neglected comb for the broders to guzzle. Other swusters went out to collect the juice of shiny black berries known to be poisonous. They poured it into empty cells for the monster to slurp at the nest entrance.

"The king opened the feast that night, bellowing for a brisket of bluebottle as his main course. The broders ordered servers to bring caterpillar casseroles, fly fillets and grasshopper gigots. They quarrelled over who would get a juicy leg or delicate wing. Afterwards, he gave a toast: *To the games and may the best broder win.*

"The party became merry as diners drained cells and called for refills. They griped at the cwen for ordering them to lay down stengers before the games got underway.

"A ring of spectators cheered and booed contestants who boxed and wrestled. The spoiled honey soon took effect, making heads tipsy. Fighting broke out between rival supporters to cause a rumpus of revolving legs and flapping wings. The bees collapsed from exhaustion into a long snooze too deep to feel the king kicking them. Finally, the king crumpled on the heap of bodies. The time arrived for the swusters to grab the stengers from the pile."

The audience raised their feelers in jubilation at the fall of the drones. They thought the story had reached its climax, but Sage had only reached half-way.

"The cwen watched from the nest entrance for the black and white-striped face of the Mangeapis, camouflaged in the slanted shadows of moonlight between trees. She worried if the broders woke too soon there would be no moral victory. They must defeat the foe to prove themselves more worthy of carrying weapons.

"The tree shuddered without warning from the force of a heavy body lunging at the trunk. The cwen staggered back to avoid a slobbering pink tongue swishing back and forth over the front row of cells.

"She waited until its eyes glazed over to ensure the monster had drunk enough of the toxic juice. Then, raising a stenger, she commanded the first wave of flyers to attack:

'Tally-ho! Let's wallop the monster.'

"The Mangeapis snarled back. Its thick hide resisted their short stengs except on its bare belly, where it hardly felt pricks. Seeing futile efforts, the cwen circled for a new target. She launched into a narrow cavity on the side of its head, barely wide enough to enter. The passage inside made a single bend before ending at a thin wall. She stabbed it several times before making a rapid exit.

"The monster roared from agonising pain and shook its head from side to side before tumbling off the branch and rolling on the ground, howling hideously. The swusters lined up in rows at the entrance, waiting for it to die, but it stood on all fours and tottered off into the night. Bees have kept watch for generations but never seen a monster like it again."

Sage paused for listeners to discuss the drama over a refreshment break. Most acclaimed the queen as a hero, but a minority thought she wronged her husband by deceiving him. A grumpy bee called the story pure fiction, which brought Hyacinth to her feet.

"What does it matter if she made it up or if monsters don't exist? It still makes a good lesson."

"It's ludicrous to imagine a broder owning a stenger. They were always bumbling wusses," the grouchy bee declared.

The obstinacy rattled Hyacinth to make another fierce reply. "Even if something doesn't happen in real life, it can still be true."

Sundew smiled at a wise friend who made them think. She looked around to see if Deadnettle heard the smears against his brethren but was told that none of the broders were allowed in the assembly. After the break, the audience returned to their places for the tale to soar to another climax.

"When the broders roused from sleep, they found themselves surrounded by armed swusters. The king snarled when the cwen approached him, brandishing a stenger to accuse him of failing to protect them.

"He denied breaking any customs, claiming ancient entitlements to royal privilege and immunity from prosecution. But nothing stands forever. He refused to accept a kingship whittled down to a ceremonial role, so the cwen declared, 'You have decided your fate and must find your own way in the Wide World. You are banished.'

"That ended the rule of a tyrant and the reign of kings forever."

The small bee in the front row stood up again, causing a hubbub by interrupting the speech. Sage stood aside to wait for the uproar to die down. The grouchy bee bawled and Hyacinth fidgeted on her feet, puffing through her spiracles.

"It's that hive poet again, Daisy. She's impulsive and has no sense of decorum."

"Don't be hard on her, Hyacinth. A bee with an artistic

temperament wants to express herself, so let's listen," Daisy said.

The voices died down when the poet recited a limerick inspired on the spot by the story.

> *The old king loved to dance,*
> *Jitterbugged around in a trance.*
> *But when he hurt his wing,*
> *And someone stole his steng,*
> *The cwen sent him off to France.*

"Thank you, Rose, for a spontaneous contribution," Sage said mildly as if used to interruption.

"The king received a harsh sentence but less than capital punishment for a deposed leader. The broders also deserved to be banned from the hyf, but the cwen forgave them if they swore to be penitent and meek. She knew that mercy heals divisions, whereas revenge only feeds more wrath.

"She could have taken on the trappings of a sovereign bee but refused, choosing instead to devote her life to making baybees for securing the family's future. She said sloth and jealousy had no place in a peaceful and prosperous hyf and called the change of heart a new covenant. Bees should respect each other, regardless of their occupation or a royal appointment. As a badge of dignity, they would have personal names in future, taken from a food plant to show commitment to vegetarianism."

After Sage closed the meeting, the trio waited for the crowds to disperse before they had a private conversation. Daisy spoke first.

"Do you remember Hyacinth said stories aren't just for amusement, Dewy?"

"I feel more proud and grateful now for knowing where we came from and the struggle to be fair and orderly. It must be wonderful to have a powerful effect on listeners. I wish I could be a storyteller like her."

"There you go again, Dewy," said Daisy. "You haven't learned to be modest after your brief superstardom. But hush, Sage is coming this way." It didn't seem like a chance encounter.

"I thought I saw you in the back row," Sage said, walking ahead of a group fanning out behind. "I hope you understand the Beeattitudes better after hearing the tale." She looked peeved at Sundew's vacant expression.

"Well, it seems I need to explain. The first of three is Love. Of course, it's easy to love swusters who love you back, but the old cwen embraced the despised broders too."

"How can I like Hawbrods after they sent me to the vault?" Sundew asked.

"Then, I have to say your love isn't strong enough. I

hope you do better at the second Beeattitude, namely Duty, something even kings are subject to."

"Hmm. I almost lost everything by strictly obeying leaders."

"You should make better choices about who to follow. It's time to stop making excuses and take Courage. That's the third Beeattitude. If you embrace the first two, you'll find the courage to fight for your family and not whinge about working hard."

"You make combat sound like a virtue, but I thought Cwen Goldenrod was a pacifist. I don't mean to be rude, but you puzzle me."

"There's a time for combat, and not necessarily physical violence, but the final goal is peace. When our Modor came as a refugee from the fire, she had to win over hyf residents who didn't want her. It took peace, patience and perseverance to build a united family. Will you be a peacemaker? She's not far away if you are ready to pledge."

A huddle of attendants surrounded the VIP, but Hyacinth urged Sundew not to be hasty. "Cwens can be moody. So let's postpone a meeting until memories of the Troubles have blown over."

"She's right," Daisy said. "You won't be welcome if an enemy has poisoned your reputation. Meeting your monarch needs the utmost diplomacy to avoid appearing like a rival to raise suspicion."

Too late for caution, the Bluebell came over to ask Daisy if her friend was the notorious half-queen. Worried about saying too much, Daisy said too little, so the courtier took a close look at the giant bee and sped back to the royal party. A thunderous voice commanded Sundew into the regal presence.

A throng of attendants divided to reveal the queen. She towered over them with short wings resting on a golden body swollen with eggs. The partners knew their friend resembled her, but hadn't realised how closely until their first sight of the queen.

Daisy rushed forward. "Beg your pardon, Your Majesty. May I introduce this young swuster, a champion worker and the first to come out alive from the Cryptum? My team will vouch for her."

The petition warmed Sundew's heart by proving the rift between them was mended. Daisy backed away without taking her eyes off the monarch, as demanded by protocol around royalty. The chattering stopped while the queen stared at Sundew, who stood frozen until beckoned with a feeler for a penetrating examination.

Sundew only managed to mumble a vow of loyalty as a

humble subject. She knew the royal fragrance that permeated the hive, but the intensity made her swoon at such close quarters.

Coming to her senses later, she found the pageant had departed and wondered if it had been a dream. She didn't know she had a royal blessing until workers gathered around with her friends to offer congratulations. She suddenly became popular again, and team supervisors vied to recruit her to their workplaces. Hyacinth had to step in to inform them she wasn't on the job market and lead her away.

After a dramatic day, the trio felt relieved to return to domestic work. Daisy chattered about family news, Hyacinth grumbled about the weather, and Sundew set a new target for polishing rows of cells. There was nothing to despise about life as an ordinary bee, especially when the team expressed appreciation.

"Lucky for us, she declined to take another job."

"No one sneers since her audience with the Cwen."

"No more tittle-tattle about her funny name."

The mention of her plant name triggered a memory that Hyacinth shared with Daisy.

"While using my wings to fan Sundew after she fainted, someone came up behind urging us to ask the cwen for permission to change Sundew's name. Unfortunately, I didn't see who spoke but would recognise her again from the pong."

"I heard you talking about me," Sundew said rather gruffly. "If someone is jealous, tell them I will never give my name up."

Apart from that slight tiff, the comb stayed serene with heads bobbing at work until late afternoon. The team only paused for brief conversations and choral singing with a few Hawbrods joining in. Extra effort by the giant bee put them ahead of schedule and they looked forward to the next assignment. The high spirits continued until Hyacinth's rasping voice lifted heads to see who strode up.

"You devil! We never expected to see you again." Hyacinth never looked more belligerent, and others stiffened at the sight of the newcomer. Despite a lesson of universal love by Sage, they couldn't extend it to a particular individual.

"Be more courteous since I have received a royal blessing like your fat friend," Hemlock said.

"You deserve a royal curse," Hyacinth rebuffed.

"Don't worry, Dewy. Her star has fallen," Daisy said, turning her back on the police chief. "Let's ignore her, for there's nothing she hates more."

"Come, come, we must be friends now," Hemlock said. "The Cwen exhorts us to cooperate in this new era."

"Don't trust her, Dewy."

"I bring glad tidings from the highest authority for Sunnedew. She has been granted a warrant to advance her first flight for launching at dawn tomorrow."

CHAPTER 11
A Dare in the Dark

He ought to know better, but it swelled Joe's pride to belong to a gang of older kids. Unfortunately, they had used him and then deserted at the first rumble of trouble in the orchard. Joe vowed not to repeat the mistake. Instead, he stuck to solitary hobbies more comforting and natural for an only child.

He played *Monopoly* against himself, careless which side won the board game. Nor did he need a partner to study insects, a hobby that earned him a nickname. He didn't mind being called B-Boy any more than his mum cared when people addressed her as Mrs. B. They both accepted abbreviations as signs of affection. Everyone knew his B stood for butterfly, beetle, and bug (the least charming epithet). He wasn't yet known as the Bee-Boy, still keeping that new fancy under wraps from friends.

He began collecting butterflies at age six, marvelling at their beauty and grateful they didn't sting or bite. Over the years, he collected fifty different species, pinning specimens with their labels in neat rows on a corkboard. The day he came home from making his own hive, he added a Red

Admiral to replace one that had lost its scales.

He hated to be distracted at his collection and pretended not to notice when Emily closed her book and looked over his shoulder.

"I prefer them flying," she said.

Shutting the lid on his collection was a way of telling her to mind her own business.

"Don't you get bored stuck indoors every night?" she asked.

He guessed the interruption wasn't only to make him feel guilty for killing butterflies and he waited for the wheedling to begin.

"Can you take me to the youth club tonight?"

Emily had endless attractions in London—from the cinema and swimming pool to walking on the Common and shopping at Wimbledon Village, even a lawn tennis tournament. But with fewer options in a village, youths created their own entertainment and sometimes mischief. Joe tried dismissing the request, saying she would feel like a fish out of water at the club. "It's for keeping younger kids off the street, not someone like you."

He guessed she wanted a change from another sudsy evening at home. Before dinner, his mum turned on *Coronation Street*, and the telly didn't stop glowing until the last soap opera.

"I need an excuse to go out." She eyed her aunt dozing in front of the screen with the volume turned up that drowned Emily's voice.

"The village is dead at night, and we're too young to enter the *King's Arms*."

"I've got a hunch where they hid the abbot's treasure and need company to check it out at a quiet time."

"You want me to waste time on a ludicrous idea?" Joe's bristling sent her back to the book, but he noticed she didn't turn the pages. She continued to cogitate on a scheme in her head, so he anticipated another interruption.

"I'm sure Brother Adam knows where they hid it long ago," she said.

"Gosh. I didn't know he was five hundred years old."

"Don't be idiotic! I meant after a new abbot hid it again."

"Why are you so interested in an old box that belongs to the monastery?"

"Is anything cooler than solving an ancient mystery? Imagine when archaeologists opened King Tut's tomb in the Egyptian desert. We saw the amazing exhibition in London when you were still in nappies. You have a village mystery I fancy writing about if we get to the bottom of it.

What could be a groovier than finding buried treasure from a medieval monastery? But I assure you I would only take the story and nothing else."

It irritated Joe to be cajoled into one of her schemes. Only a nut would go out on a wild goose chase at night that might land him in as much trouble as in cahoots with the gang. She looked pained when he refused point-blank to cooperate, knowing no one else she could ask.

"Sorry to beg a favour when there's not much in it for you. I want to write about the discovery for an essay competition. Even as a runner-up, it could help my application to Cambridge University for studying English Literature in a couple of years."

So that was it! She had nerve to drag him in, and it was completely unnecessary. "You already have plenty to write about, so make up the rest to avoid getting in trouble."

She gave him a horrified stare. "That *would* be trouble if I deceived the judges by sending in fiction for a non-fiction award."

She desperately needed to confirm the box existed for an essay to be taken seriously. A story left to guess-work over an unsolved mystery would be a non-starter. She asked Joe to imagine the discoverer Howard Carter leaving the door to Tut's tomb unopened and returning home to invent a story about the Pharoah's mummy. Even a glimpse at the monk's treasure would satisfy her and her readers.

The project meant too much to be given up lightly. She assured him it wouldn't be wicked to have a quick look, and promised to take the blame if caught.

"We won't lie to your mum if we tell her we're going to the club and only stay a minute before leaving. Are you worried about Brad?"

Joe shook his head. "They banned him for smoking on the premises."

"You might regret saying no because you have a personal stake from family history. Did you know your grandad took the box away from the Grattiches to put it in the rightful hands of the abbot? We ought to check if it's still safe."

So that explained why his parents didn't get along with the other family. Emily made a cunning appeal to his loyalty.

"You are as nutty as the monk. Why do you think I'd go without knowing where?"

"Okay, but you must guess before I tell."

"I suppose it's near the church hall since you want to go there."

"You should know that Catholics wouldn't hide it on

Church of England property. Here's a clue: a stone-cold bed for the dead." She found baiting him amusing.

"You can't mean the graveyard because monks wouldn't bury treasure on holy ground."

She laughed at him for sounding like his pious mother. "I will tell you since you're getting warm. I think it's nearby in the mausoleum."

"I never heard of a mouseoleum."

She giggled. "You know the little house they made for the abbot's tomb. It's such a clever place for keeping a secret, and they don't even lock the door."

The temerity of breaking into the tomb stunned him. He raked his mind for flaws. For starters, why would the monastery hide property they owned? If the box still contained valuables, why didn't they sell them to beautify the abbey or give alms to the poor? If they needed to hide it, who was in on the secret? And if his grandad knew, perhaps he told the rest of the family.

"What do you think?" she asked, impatient for an answer. "I only need you to keep watch at the door while I snoop inside."

He knew impulsive decisions are often mistaken but gave her credit for a dazzling idea. The more he thought about it, the harder he found to resist. What harm could be done? No one went there at night unless Cuthbert came back late from the tool shed, and being under her spell, he wouldn't condemn them. Older boys had already dashed to the door to fulfil the dare, although they didn't go inside. Joe's dad called it a rite of passage. Was this his son's best chance, or did the company of an older girl disqualify him?

The sun had already set when they left home with a promise to return before ten o'clock. Lights blazed at the church hall where a Shakin' Stevens record boomed through an open door into the night. A clean-cut parson stood with a hand cupped over his ear to catch the name as Joe introduced his cousin.

Joe joined his mates at the dartboard. Emily wandered

around to avoid a couple of leering lads until the pinball machine was free. As soon as it turned completely dark outside, she tapped him on the shoulder several times until he could leave after losing a winning streak.

"Hey, B-Boy," one of the lads sneered. "Is that yer mum coming to take yer 'ome for bed?"

Joe glowered back as he followed Emily out to the empty street. They had to take the boundary path because the monastery gate closed at dusk. Cool air misting over warm earth hung like a spectral veil over the fields. She complained when he turned off the torch to save the battery but agreed they saw further ahead after their eyes adjusted. Lights twinkled in the village across the meadow, and only their footfalls and chimes from the tower broke the silence.

"I didn't know it got so dark in the country. Why don't you have any street lighting? I'm not saying I'm scared." She didn't sound as confident as she spoke. The dark didn't faze Joe, though he had other qualms.

"I thought of the hullabaloo if your essay is printed. A villager might read it, and then Mum is bound to find out."

"Crikey! I never thought of that if I won the award." Emily had sailed a wild imagination like a yacht with a billowing spinnaker out of Salcombe Bay into the choppy English Channel. His words took the wind out of her sails.

"I must disguise the names of people and places or drop the project."

Joe almost felt sorry for crushing her. "Just keep my name out of it, but we've gone too far for turning back."

He strode down the path with the confidence of a sleepwalker on a familiar route and never drifted onto the grass. She walked close enough to bump elbows. They swung the gate slowly to avoid its hinges screeching.

They had never visited in the dark before; it looked a different place, and no street sounds to break the peace. A half-moon emerged from behind a bank of clouds to cast a silvery light over memorial stones and crosses. They steeled across the yard as cautiously as if stalking game animals.

When the mausoleum loomed into view, the door looked like a black void instead of solid wood, and shadows concealed the sculpted pair of cherubs. Joe tapped his knuckles on the door.

"What are you doing? There's no one inside. Or do you believe in ghosts?" Emily whispered. She couldn't see in the torchlight a grin on his face as he pictured his dad giving a thumbs-up for coming.

She fumed at the bolt from tugging at it vainly, "Blast. It won't budge, so you try."

Joe bashed it with a rock. It sounded loud enough to

wake sleepers in flats over the High Street. After the rude din, they waited for stillness to return before a second try made the bolt shoot back. The door grated open to stick halfway, leaving barely enough space for a teenager or skinny monk to squeeze inside.

"I'll keep watch here," he said, not a gallant offer but the deal they agreed.

"The one with the strongest light should go first," she said. "I'll wait here if you light my candle with your match." Her face glowed from a flame dancing in her breath like a living thing and friend of chilled nerves on the threshold of the dead.

Joe peered through the doorway into a darkness as deep as a cave. Then, holding the torch at arm's length, he flashed it around to glimpse the interior.

Emily stepped back, her voice quaking, "Let's go home if you don't see anything."

He huffed before sidling inside. The beam shone more orange than yellow on the bare walls of the room the size of his bedroom. A stone slab as long as his bed filled most of the floor, presumably to cover the abbot's coffin. It reminded him of a sarcophagus at Wells Cathedral, except for the absence of a carved figure on top. He felt Emily's warm breath on his neck.

"Let's not hang about," she insisted. "I'm getting cold."

"Wait! I can see fallen petals and leaves around a glass vase. Someone left a bunch of flowers." He swung the light to the far end of the slab, straining to make out another object. The light shrank to a faintly glowing filament in the bulb. Shaking the torch had no effect, so she held out the candle for him to check the battery inside.

Then her piercing scream made him jog the candle out of her hand. The flame died on the ground, extinguishing the only light source.

"Sorry! I felt something run over my foot." The exclamation echoed in the chamber. "I had a wrong hunch, so let's scram."

He needed no urging after they folded into a blackness that made them invisible. He slammed the door but couldn't push the bolt all the way.

Falling into each other's arms after rushing back to the gate, they laughed aloud between deep breaths. She talked about the youth club along the path, more for the comfort of imagining bright lights and gaiety until they reached the lane.

"At least we can rule that out," she said, without a hint of regret. "I need to think of a craftier hiding place."

"But I saw something else on the slab. A small box—"

"A what—?" She halted them by grabbing his arm. "You better explain."

"I couldn't see it properly."

"Why didn't you say before? Did you deliberately keep it from me?"

Emily blamed him for bringing a dud battery, and he grumbled back for dropping the candle. Unfortunately, they couldn't return without a torch, and she needed time to make another plan. Meantime, she looked forward to the consolation of cosying in an armchair with her novel, while all Joe wanted was a mug of hot cocoa before bed.

CHAPTER 12
Maiden Flight

A breeze from the field smelled fragrant after the overnight rain. Shuffling wings inside the hive told of bees waking for another workday. They descended to the entrance where Sundew waited with Daisy for flight instructions.

She hardly contained her excitement waiting to beat wings to her flower. She had never seen beyond the hedges walling the meadow, only known to field bees on peregrinations up to three miles from home. The only sour note for the trip was the escort assigned to her, the same who took her to the Cryptum.

Daisy brushed her friend's wings. "I asked around about your flower, but still no one has heard of it."

"Your flowers are dotted all over the meadow; I prefer the mystery of not knowing what mine is like. If my name means anything, I expect sunnedews have a crown of golden petals and glistening leaves."

A familiar voice hailed them from the throng piling out of the hive for departing flights. "Good morning, folks. It's a fine day for a graduation."

The pair held Hemlock in too much contempt to make

a polite reply. Sundew waited at the launch pad, impatient to leave the hated police chief behind.

"How will I identify my plant?" she asked. "Is it a kind of sunflower?"

A puzzled look revealed that even Hemlock didn't know what it looked like.

"I've seen it, boss," Shady said. "It's a cute plant that lives in damp places."

"I want to go with my friend," Daisy butted in. "My launch date isn't far off."

"Certainly not, Forty-Seven. You don't qualify for special treatment or need to go far for a daisy. Be prepared to miss your team mate for a while."

Shady haw-hawed quietly to herself.

"I insist on going part of the way."

Hemlock narrowly saved her job during the harmonisation of society after the Troubles, so she couldn't push Daisy around too much.

"I will allow one flight around the field together, then back to work you go."

The landing strip became busy with flyers lining up to take off into the brightening sky. After warming their muscles and folding legs, they flew in every direction. Sundew thought it would be easy.

Daisy got aloft first. She circled the hive at a safe distance from the rush hour traffic. "Come on, Dewy, it's wonderful up here."

Sundew's feet clawed the wooden board like anchors, despite her frantically flapping wings. The sight made the police laugh at the formerly proud bee. Her little wings cut her down to size, more decorative than airworthy. To be grounded is a grave handicap, condemning bees to house duties or a worse fate.

Flying in tight circles, Daisy urged her to keep trying and ignore the taunts. But buzzing wings and jumping up and down only slightly increased Sundew's elevation before she bumped down on her feet again.

Daisy landed to check her friend's wings. "I can't see any problem. You must believe we are born to fly."

"Don't laugh if my wings are too short."

"You mustn't give up. Breathe in deeply through your spiracles and imagine zooming over a wildflower field."

Sundew's wings went into a blur at two-hundred beats per second; the membranes would shatter if any faster. She suddenly noticed her feet didn't feel the board anymore and soon had the exhilaration of ascending like a helicopter.

Worried about getting burnt by flying too close to the

sun, she stifled her muscle motors for a level flight across the field and back. Although glad to hear her friend clapping, she knew it fell short of an ace performance. Sundew was far more confident travelling on the ground than in the air, more like a truck than a flashy F-16 jet. But size had the compensation of endurance on a long-haul flight.

The friends headed straight to the garden, disobeying Hemlock's order. They were eager to see the place foragers advertised in the hive by performing rave dances. They marvelled at the borders blushing with rainbow colours. The only unadorned sight was a stone hive in the distance where the keeper lived.

Hemlock griped for making her wait for them to return. "I would clip your wings if you weren't already scheduled for a journey."

"Have a safe trip, Dewy, and don't forget to bring a sample of that special pollen to show the team," Daisy said with a wave.

Before the deputy departed, Hemlock advised her not to push the new graduate too hard. Words sounding kindly were really intended to be a snub. Sundew followed Shady over the hedge and across acres of yellow flowers glowing in the sun, recently risen over purple hills. She had thought there could be no finer scenery anywhere in the world than in her neighbourhood. Still, the flight began to break that notion with dreams of adventure.

Beyond the fields of crops and grazing animals, they reached a wasteland where thousands of flowers bobbed rings of yellow petals, each bearing a central fuzz of pollen-coated stamens.

Eureka, she thought and floated down to join hoverflies and day-flying moths on the bounty. But she steered away when Shady growled that her plant didn't grow on a sandy heath.

Her escort became irritable from the slow progress and flew extra circuits until she caught up. Seeing Sundew puffing for air, Shady allowed her to rest on a spike of flowers. After an unsteady landing, she tumbled into one of the bells as a larger body might fall down a shallow well. She emerged wet and covered in yellow dust. *Aha! So that's how we gather ingredients for making bee bread.* She didn't know that every time a forager visits a flower it exchanges pollen to fertilise them for producing seeds.

A larger, louder and furrier kind of bee than a drone peered out of an adjacent bell, buzzing with indignation.

"This is humblebee territory, and bathing here in nectar is strictly forbidden."

"Begging your pardon, ma'am. I'm searching for a sunnedew."

"This is a foxglove. Don't they teach you anything useful in hyf classes nowadays?"

Sundew left in humiliation to find Shady, but the deputy had vanished. She pined for the guide, alarmed at being alone and adrift in an unknown land.

A long green insect startled her by leaping out of the grass. It unfolded a ridiculously long leg to rub against its body for playing a tune. After the grasshopper finished a monotonous serenade, it mumbled in a foreign language and sprang away.

The first encounter with a new insect had been embarrassing, the second entertaining, but the next was scary. An aerial acrobat with gigantic eyes twisted and turned to pursue a cloud of gnats. Luckily, Sundew's colour camouflaged her on the dirt.

Shady reappeared and bragged about her hearty breakfast but wouldn't allow Sundew to eat until they reached the destination.

After the heathland, they followed a river winding between fields and woods with a salty breeze in their faces from a distant estuary. Bleached tree skeletons rotted from roots that had drowned in a winter flood on an inside bend.

Mosses and slippery liverworts gleamed in the poorly drained sod. The guide evidently knew the place because she flew straight to a clump of golden globes.

Sundew expected to be waved over but the deputy jeered instead.

"Don't look hungrily at marsh marigolds, which are my plants. Yours are over there."

Shady seemed too bad-tempered to deserve the name of a pretty plant. But why did she point at small, dingy flowers dangling on frail plants with lower buds still in wrappers?

Sundew ignored them to search elsewhere.

"Go back to your plants," the deputy shouted.

"They can't be sunnedews"

The deputy spoke the truth this time. Reluctantly, Sundew flew closer before making a tricky landing on one of the petite flowers. Its stem bowed under her weight, almost tipping her into the bog. She heard sniggering.

"Never mind if there's little pollen on the stamens. You can guzzle as much yummy nectar on the leaves as you like."

Only knowing about plants from hearsay, Sundew didn't realise it is rare for them to make the same liquor on leaves as flowers use to attract pollinators. The ring of spoon-shaped leaves at the base of the stem had a dense covering of tiny red tentacles tipped with glinting globules. She thought the resemblance to dewdrops explained the name of the plant that looked contemptible in every other respect.

Shady bellowed as she hesitated again. "Hurry up and take your refreshment. I must return soon for other duties."

The stem pinged upright when she descended on a leaf to drool over scrumptious droplets. A cry from a rolled-up leaf nearby made her withdraw her tongue before sucking. She knew leaves grow, breathe, feed, and fall in due season like animals, but had never heard of them talking.

"Please help," pleaded a faint voice. "I'm a poor fly trapped on leaf hairs and smothering to death."

Sundew understood the dialect of a distant relative. She couldn't ignore the appeal after her experience as a prisoner, despite the disgusting reputation of flies.

"Don't worry. I'll release you."

But when she tried to walk, her legs stuck to hairs that refused to let go. As bad as it was, she hadn't touched them with her tongue. Shady cruised nearby to check the leaf had pinioned her.

"Have you lost your appetite for breakfast after becoming a plant's lunch?" She made a cruel he-he-he laugh and flew off.

A dumb plant with a noble-sounding name had trapped Sundew. She felt a fool again after being duped into the Cryptum. Had she recalled the story of the queen who used a poisonous plant against an enemy, she might have approached the sundew more cautiously. But she assumed out of innocence that every plant is friendly to bees, so it came as a shock to discover the benevolent sun allows evil trickery in a beautiful world.

If she didn't escape, her friends wouldn't know what misfortune had befallen her, and the vengeful police would never tell. Struggling to get free only aggravated her plight. Every time she touched another hair, it added to those clinging tenaciously to her. When the fly stopped blubbering in its leafy tomb, Sundew abandoned hope for herself. The leaf curled over her like a tortilla wrapped around a filling. But she wouldn't be fast food for a sundew because insect prey marinates in leafy juices first.

CHAPTER 13
Pity the Critters

Joe and Emily counted twelve chimes on the clock tower as they sauntered through the garden. They timed their arrival for when the monks went to Mass and tourists had lunch at Betsy's Tea Shoppe. Emily walked casually beside Joe, who waved a butterfly net to conceal their real intent. Seated on the graveyard bench where she had chatted to Cuthbert a few days earlier, the cousins looked around warily to check if anyone followed. The mausoleum looked less forbidding in bright sunshine.

Emily on tenterhooks scolded Joe in whispers, "You should've told me this is a better time. Then we could have avoided a fright in the night."

He would have thrown back the blame, except arguments never settled anything. "Did you remember the camera?" he asked.

She patted a trouser pocket. "Keep a lookout. This won't take long."

He watched her casually approach the little building, pretending to read headstones before sneaking around the side. She reappeared seconds later, scowling and sat down.

"He padlocked it. Probably found the candle, or because you didn't secure the bolt."

"Do you think he knows?"

"Why should he suspect us? I'm mad we got so close, and now there's a fat chance of seeing that box."

He left her alone until she suggested a country walk to lessen the disappointment. Climbing over a stile at the bottom of the meadow, they followed the signpost to Bluebottom Wood.

"Maybe I can find wildflowers for your mum's birthday. Did you forget it's tomorrow?"

The path ran alongside a field where a tractor chugged along straight rows. It sprayed the crop from twin booms extending from a tank behind the cab.

"It doesn't just kill weevils," Joe muttered. He knew that butterflies would be scarce all summer within a mile of the killing fields.

"That's rich coming from you."

He swooped his net wildly at the verge to express irritation with the criticism. When it caught in a plant, he yanked the stick and hauled out purple, bell-shaped flowers.

"Don't touch them! It's a belladonna, or you probably call it deadly nightshade," Emily exclaimed.

The name sounded familiar: didn't an ancient philosopher die from drinking the poisonous juice?

"If you don't die from swallowing the berries, they give you hallucinations. Who would think it's in the potato family?"

"Why aren't spuds deadly?" He hoped to trap her into admitting she didn't know, but his next question was genuinely curious. "I wonder if honey made from nightshade makes us sick?"

"Perhaps bees are too smart to visit those flowers. You should ask the monk, but don't eat honey unless you know where it comes from."

The path came to a dead-end at a remnant of ancient woodland where Joe knew a hole in the fence. Gnarled oaks and stately beeches towered over thickets of hazel or holly and fleshy plants carpeted the ground.

"I hoped to find lots of bluebells." Emily frowned as if the signpost deceived her.

"I thought you would know they are over by June, but there are bunches of yellow flowers on Blackfriar's Bog."

Before they left the wood, a pheasant rose from cover in an explosion of heavy wings and a grating call that startled her. Joe shrugged to express what he thought.

They climbed over a fence into a cattle field. She

snapped pictures of the valley where a river divided deep green pastures as it meandered towards the coast.

Joe scouted the fence line for the rope he remembered strung between trees. It bowed under the weight of carcasses hanging by their necks or legs. On catching up with him, Emily stepped back in horror and held her nose while swatting flies with the other hand.

"I never saw a more gruesome sight. What does it mean?"

"Haven't you seen a gamekeeper's gibbet before?"

"Who would be so cruel?"

"The gamekeeper shoots and traps predators of game birds and their nests on Sir Renard Huntley's estate. Old Grattich doesn't give a fig about owls, badgers or other protected species. The area is closed for a pheasant shoot in November."

Emily thought aloud of the English countryside in *Winnie-the-Pooh* and *The Wind in the Willows*. The walk shattered her idyll of rural life, more violent than the big city.

He called out the names of the bundles of fur and feathers along the line clouded with flies. "He got a jay, a buzzard, several crows, a weasel, and two squirrels. I think the black fur is the remains of a mole."

"Oh, not Moley, the kindest creature on the *River Bank* and a friend of Ratty."

"He didn't get my Ferdie," said Joe. "My ferret escaped that I took rabbiting with Dad."

"You country bumpkins are a bloodthirsty breed. I bet you never read *Watership Down*." Emily stalked away, leaving him to regret a blunder for forgetting that she had a fancy breed of bunnies in a hutch at home.

Wandering downhill with his net poised, he kept alert for butterflies and avoided stepping on sloppy mines dropped by cows. He came back to find her sitting astride a five-bar gate.

"Look what I caught!" He lifted his hand out of the net to show a sky-blue butterfly.

A frown said it all: *Is that your latest victim?*

"Look at the streamer on the back wings. It's a Long-tailed Blue blown by a gale across the Channel from France. It's very rare."

"Congratulations on another specimen for your collection." Emily turned to show disdain. He had let it go on looking back, but the hand she laid on his shoulder he brusquely pushed off.

Sitting cross-legged in the shade of a hedge, she took out a small notebook to scribble sentences. He sprawled in the sunshine with his eyes closed. After a while, he plucked a blade of grass to blow between his thumbs, making a painful screech. She ignored the impatient call to leave, although glad to get his attention.

"I've gone back to fiction where I'm not chained by facts. Talking about poisonous honey gave me an idea." She launched the story before he could object.

"It's about a warlock called Erlingur, a hermit who foraged for forest food and craved for something sweet to eat. Finding a nest of ferocious black bees, he cast a spell on them for safely taking honey made from purple flowers. It tasted sweeter than candy and blacker than soot—"

"I never heard of killer bees making black honey."

"Pay attention and don't side-track me. The warlock bartered for bread in the castle marketplace, where peasants looked suspiciously at his black robe embroidered with pentacles. As he munched a trencher of bread dripping with black honey, he could read the future on their faces when they stared at him. A girl changed into a woman in a wedding dress, and a man developed the angry rash of smallpox. Each vision evaporated when he lost the taste.

"When a man in chainmail appeared, he took a fresh lick of honey. The knight dissolved into a ghostly image who plunged his sword into the chest of the castle's custodian, Baron Ragnar. Erlingur pointed his ebony stick to accuse him of plotting treason. The high-ranking knight persuaded guards to bundle him into the dungeon to be burnt to death for witchcraft the next day—"

"What do you think, Joe? Joe! I know you are pretending to fall asleep. Don't tell me it's boring."

He turned over to yawn and covered his eyes from the sun. "It sounds like an old-fashioned fairy story."

She should have known he would say something damning, but then he shocked her by making a close guess about the rest of the story.

"He will magic himself out of jail to rescue a pretty damsel before she's forced to marry the knight—or something like that. Why don't you write the bees' story instead of using them as the warlock's power source? Don't you feel sorry for stealing their honey?"

"Hmm. It's funny that you would take the bee's point of view. I'll think about it."

After crossing a heath of prickly gorse, they walked along a river bank between water meadows to a stand of rotted tree stumps.

"You didn't warn me it would be muddy here." Emily grimaced at the chocolate goo around her tennis shoes.

"You wanted bog flowers." Joe pointed at a clump of marsh marigolds.

She skirted a shallow pool to gather a posy while he stooped to examine the prints of a fox. Then, noticing a cluster of small plants with rolled-up leaves among the mosses, he called her to identify them.

"I can't remember the name, but I'm certain they are carnivorous plants. They eat bugs to get the nourishment that's missing in poor soil."

He wished he had brought a magnifying lens for a close examination of the red hairs covering the upper surfaces of leaves. They reminded him of the ball-tipped bristles on his mother's hairbrush, except their size fitted tiny people in *The Borrowers*.

"If you know so much about botany, you should write science fiction. I might enjoy your story if it's about man-eating lettuces terrorising the London suburbs to get their own back on cruel salad-eaters." He giggled at the image of vengeful vegetables chasing his cousin along the capital's streets.

"Someone has already published it. He called the plants triffids."

Moisture oozed on Joe's jeans from kneeling on moss as he opened his pocket knife to loosen soil around rootlets to lift one of the plants out intact.

"Now I've got a birthday present for her," he said. "Mum won't grumble about flies in the house anymore."

"I love the idea, but she will still need a flyswatter."

They put the plant in a flowerpot from the greenhouse and pinched off untidy leaves to make it presentable. The first leaf had unrolled to show an insect's exoskeleton on its surface. The second one was still rolled up, so Joe transferred it to Emily's palm. She dropped it.

"Eek! I felt it move."

Prised open between his dirty fingernails, he found a large bee immobilised on leaf hairs. The insect didn't resist as he pared it off the leaf.

"It's big enough for a queen but shouldn't be out in a hostile world. See the wound on its back, Emmy? I think something happened to it before getting caught. Let's keep it to show the monk."

He slid it into a jam jar with a dab of honey and placed it on a shelf over his bed. Then he hurried downstairs for a fish-and-chip supper his mum brought home wrapped in newspaper.

"I remember now," Emily said, shaking a cruse of vinegar over her battered haddock. "You can tell her the plant is a sundew."

The sound of dustbins banging in the back of a growling truck woke Joe early the following day. Instead of burying his head under the covers, he sprang out of bed to dress and bring the flowerpot indoors. Seeing the jar missing from the bookshelf, he leaned over the balustrade to shout, "Happy birthday, Mum. I'll be down in a jiffy when I've found something I left on the shelf yesterday."

"If you mean that dirty jar, the bin men took it away."

"Aah! I won't find an insect like that again."

CHAPTER 14
Second Birth

Sundew lay in the jar with leaf hairs sticking all over her body. Nobody would call her beautiful now, but she didn't care about appearances anymore. Perhaps no other bee had faced so many hazards in so short a time. And now, after she set off hopefully, her journey ended in a glass prison after being captured by a flesh-eating plant.

She dragged her feet towards a whiff of honey for its energy and comfort. Before finishing the dregs, a violent shaking tossed her in the air, giving a momentary sensation of weightlessness before she slammed down to roll over. A glimmer of light gave a faint prospect of release before closing in darkness again.

The shallow sleep she fell into from fatigue broke as soon as the shaking returned with the deafening roar of an engine. Bracing her feet on the glass base for more episodes kept her steady until a tremendous crash left her dazed and upside down. After the ordeal, the stillness gave her solace until the dread of abandonment bore down. She cowered on the prison floor and thought, *So this is what it feels like to die alone.*

Frozen in despair, she wondered how the ordeal would end. Water trickling over her feet made her step aside to a drier place and brush past a glass shard. Moving further, the air felt warmer and moister, though it stank. With a clearer head, she would have known sooner the jar had cracked open in the last crash. She had left the prison.

The freedom to crawl away gave her a fresh impulse for living. *I might survive if I can see Sunne again.* Without a highway through a jungle of rubbish, she squeezed through winding channels, past jumbles of paper bundles, smelly cans and rotting vegetables. If the mound was a giant anthill, a honeybee could teach the residents a lesson on how to build a sweet and hygienic home. Some paths through the maze ended in cul-de-sacs, forcing her to backtrack. Nevertheless, she made progress, and when a channel split to offer a choice, she obeyed the urge to take the higher road.

The sound of whirring wings made her heart beat faster. Although it was an alien rhythm, she yearned to meet other creatures, and almost anyone would do. Around the next corner, three bluebottles hummed contentedly on a roasted chicken carcass. She couldn't join the revolting feast despite an empty stomach, so she begged for honey.

"You spoiled brat. Eat what you find or starve on foolish dreams," one of the flies told her.

She plodded onward and upward, still craving for food, company and light. The ascent seemed endless, so there were no words to match the joy of seeing the first crack of sunlight ahead except thanks for the sun's rays.

As she emerged from the heap, the air smelled fresher. A carpet of green fields dotted with trees beckoned her, but she had to dry her wings first without attracting attention from strange animals roaming the top. A hairy critter with a skinny tail scuttled past with a sliver of doughnut in its goofy teeth. A cockroach vied with ants for ownership of a hulled orange. And a scary pair of black feathery creatures had a tug-of-war over a slice of bread. In that repulsive menagerie, everybody cared for themselves, and everything smelled disgusting. Upon getting airborne, Sundew shook the last withered plant hairs off her wings.

Spying a sunflower field ahead, she flew to the first bloom to plan a triumphant homecoming. Her co-workers would be as engrossed by her travels as they were by Sage's stories. She didn't care if they called her maiden flight invalid for coming home without pollen.

Without familiar landmarks or scents as guides, she asked local bees for directions to shelter before sundown. They warned her not to camp in the open but didn't invite her hospitality.

Her luck changed when another traveller gave a friendly wave. It resembled a honeybee in size and shape except for its skinhead and black stripes on a yellow jacket. A pair of stubby feelers twitched incessantly, giving the impression of intelligence. A shared language meant they were cousins and, therefore, more trustworthy. The insect introduced herself as Spike, not known as a plant name.

Spike offered overnight lodging in her family's nest, as surprising as it was irresistible after honeybees turned down her request. The pair hadn't gone far before Spike flew down to join a picnic with her relatives, an ill-mannered bunch too busy slurping food to notice them. Sundew shuddered as the insects buried their heads in a stinking cadaver that a large predator had left half-eaten.

"Don't you like meat? You need animal protein to be strong." Spike looked aghast as she turned up her feelers at the invitation to join the scavengers. She told her sisters they would have a vegetarian guest staying that night.

When the gang finished stuffing themselves, they gathered the scraps to take home for storage. Sundew hoped they had some pollen bread in the pantry for breakfast before she resumed her journey.

Spike lived in a rustic nest suspended from a tree branch. Her family didn't need keepers to construct it with wood fibres they chewed into paper discs for glueing onto walls. It had a neat entrance hole.

Ushered inside, Sundew perched on a ledge to study a community that only partly resembled her own. Hundreds of workers and a few drones milled around the reception area. They had nursery cells for raising larvae, but a pantry reeking of decayed flesh had no honeycomb. She guessed her hosts were a primitive tribe of bees who eked out a living by hunting and gathering. They hadn't learned the value of manufactured food that stays wholesome for ages.

When Spike announced the stranger she brought home *for* dinner, Sundew thought she really meant *to* dinner. Perhaps out of tiredness, she forgot Spike had already told them she had declined an evening meal. The family gathered around to be introduced: the ring of fierce faces looked like a troupe of clowns in loud stripes.

They stepped forward, in turn, to sniff her with wiry feelers, a customary greeting for insects, although the intensity seemed vulgar. Some came up behind to stroke her wings, and others impudently licked her wax gland.

After one thanked Spike for bringing them a 'sweet and fat dessert', Sundew began to wonder whether it was a joke or a slip of the tongue.

Had gullibility led her into peril again? She couldn't fight off so many insects, and the crowd blocked the exit. So she asked to meet their queen, hoping for the same kind of gracious reception as from her own monarch. Instead, she only heard a ripple of sniggering.

She had met devious and obnoxious characters before, but how would she manage a gang of thugs on their home ground? They looked like brigands hungering for bounty.

"You are a perfidious bug!" she cursed Spike.

One of them jumped on her back from behind to grasp a wing between its mandibles. A torn wing would leave her helpless. The crowd roared approval at the cowardly act, and nobody rooted for her as a contest began.

Shaking from side to side made the opponent more determined. It manoeuvred to a strike position, and Sundew curled in response to protect her abdomen. She hadn't always prided herself in greater size and strength because it generated envy. But her life now depended on every advantage she possessed to compensate for a lack of combat experience. She threw the body off like a tight spring that releases its energy without warning.

The opponents circled each other for a chance to gain from the other's hesitation. However, finding herself in a fight to the death jarred with Sundew's pledge to be non-violent in future. The only consolation for conflicted feelings was remembering Daisy assuring her that force is justified against implacable enemies.

Her opponent had greater agility. After jumping on again and pinning her down, it strained to bring its sting close enough to strike. Although she couldn't see, Sundew realised the danger as the observers cheered louder and waved their feelers.

After taking a deep breath, she flung the body off again, which landed upside down, beating its legs in the air. Supporters ran to help their champion on its feet, but she pushed them aside to jab one of its black stripes. Bees have an acidic poison as potent by injection as wasp's alkaline mixture. The attacker's legs thrashed around before going into a spasm and then stilled. Sundew had never killed anyone before: it didn't feel good, although she had no choice.

She expected the onlookers to rush forward and overpower her, but they only watched, as if expecting her to die next. Perhaps they heard a rumour that stinging is a mortal injury for honeybees. She knew it is lethal to yank out barbs embedded in the skin of hairy animals because the guts come out with it. But she had met veterans who had safely withdrawn stings after impaling the cuticles of insect adversaries and not harmed themselves. So stinging wasn't always suicidal.

Moreover, not all stings were the same. The queen had a long smooth shaft for repeated service without hurting herself. Sundew slid her sting into its abdominal quiver after checking her innards were still in place. The wasted seconds cost her the chance to escape before another gladiator came forward, this time to challenge a duel.

They started by facing in opposite directions before reversing into each other with stings elevated. Voices rose in excitement as the gap closed. Her opponent received constant advice to stay on target, while she had to count steps to know when in strike range. Swishing her weapon from side to side like a sabre, she thrust it on feeling the first contact. After brief resistance from the cuticle, it glided inside the body, and she squeezed poison out the tip to paralyse its nerves and muscles. The gasping audience confirmed she scored again before she saw the slain body.

Expecting them to surge forward, she launched immediately with muscles warmed by exercise. Seeing a circle of light, she zoomed out while they bumped against each in the narrow channel, trying to be the first to follow.

On catching up with her, they dive-bombed but couldn't deflect the heavyweight from her beeline, whose glands poured extra hormones to boost stamina and determination. After the pursuers gave up the chase, she throttled back to cruising speed. However, lonesome feelings crept in to replace the ecstasy of escape. The sight of daisies on lawns triggered flashbacks to friends. What would Daisy say if she could see her now?

Leaving the lawns behind, Sundew flew to the first fallow field and landed on a blue cornflower. She had travelled far enough for one day, and the sun already burned crimson on the horizon.

"Psst, don't trespass on private property, big bee." The high-pitched voice came from a fierce little bee with a metallic blue sheen perched on an adjacent flower. It tried to shoo her off before she could suck the flower's nectary. Sundew wanted to avoid strife after the recent skirmish, although reluctant to fly in fading light.

"Please let me stay for a night. I'm exhausted after fighting yellow-jacketed bees."

"Ooh! You are a sucker if you fell among them and don't know the difference between bees and waesps. If I make you an exception, I want you gone at dawn. Don't behave like a relative who invites herself for a day and drags it out to a fortnight. Hard enough to put up with neighbours dropping by, but guests are insufferable. They don't leave a host in peace, always wanting to chat and share a meal. I don't care if anyone teases me for being a recluse as long as they respect my solitude."

Sundew had never heard of a hermit's life before and couldn't see the point of living without the conversation and cooperation found in a community. Nevertheless, she gladly accepted the terms of the little bee, the first to show her kindness that day.

"I'm a hunigbee called Sunnedew on my way home to Goldenham."

"You're a strange one with an unlucky name. They call me Amma, the same as all my relatives."

The name flummoxed Sundew, not the meaning of it but the blurring of personal identity. She had felt proud the day she dropped the anonymous 'newbie' for a unique name that gave dignity for standing out from the masses. "Do you belong to an identical clone?" she asked, hoping it wouldn't offend the little bee.

Amma scoffed at the ignorance. She said mason bees have mothers and fathers like other bees but otherwise live independently. They didn't need fancy names or titles when one could serve for all.

"Why make life more complicated than necessary? Living apart, we rarely see relatives and never fumble to remember a name if we bump into one by mistake. Nor can we fall out with anyone as you do in a family. The solitary life is a blissful existence."

Sundew struggled to avoid becoming angry at the criticism of everything most precious to her. "We are a happy bunch working together for the common good. We get on better now with a brod that shares our hyf."

"Aha! Just as I thought, arguments over property and personal antagonisms create unhappiness that grows into bitter resentment. I don't need company or to share anything. Besides, you can't be true to yourself if decisions are made by a majority. Don't kid yourself you can ever be an independent thinker or a radical voice because others formed you."

Sundew had never met anyone so sure of herself. Amma saw all the pitfalls of society and none of its benefits. How could someone who never left home be so confident in her own opinions? She lived in a bubble, only able to see her own reflection and nothing of the world outside. By shunning society, she forfeited the benefits of wise elders like Sage.

"Your hyfs are more trouble than they're worth. By building bigger nurseries, you become overcrowded and stuff pantries with food that encourages greed and envy. When I am hungry, I dine *al fresco* on seasonal food and don't need winter supplements. I don't ask for home deliveries or dancers for directions to fine eating. Nor do my kind need nurses. I close each baybee unit behind a mud wall in a plant stem with a food package for when they hatch."

"Is it possible to be a solo parent?" Sundew looked astonished. "We need cwens to make baybees—"

The sound of a *boing, boing* turned their attention to a hefty bumblebee. A burly bee bounced on a silk trampoline that sent an orb spider scuttling and whining about the damage.

"If we keep quiet, the busybody may not see us," Amma hissed.

They watched it tear sticky cobwebs off its body. A different species to the grumpy bumblebee seen earlier, this bee looked like an insect equivalent of a pudgy honey bear in a black-and-orange coat. The mason bee sighed when her second visitor ambled over.

"I thought I saw you had company, Amma, and

couldn't miss a special event. Please introduce her."

Amma looked glum as Bombi shuffled to be comfortable on another flower. "This Sunnedew has odd views about society and cwens, although you have some in common."

"Don't be boorish," the bumblebee rebuked.

"You colonial bees have boring jobs and bossy rulers. You fawn over your privileged royalty and tolerate scrounging broders. But look at me, a jack of all trades and cwen of my realm, admittedly a tiny dominion, but all I want or need. I don't make honey or a wax mansion, yet I never go hungry and am snug at night. Simplicity is the key to a happy life."

"Don't be taken in by her clever talk, Sunnedew. Her humdrum life would be empty of news and history if I didn't stop by."

"Blah, blah, blah." Amma resented them ganging up and would have left except she didn't want them to win the argument. "Did a history lesson ever stop the repetition of a past mistake? You won't enjoy the present if you dwell on old miseries. I advise living for the day and forgetting the past."

Sundew couldn't stay silent at the mockery of her ancestors' contributions. "You're wrong, Amma. We learn from each other how to improve society and save lives. I've seen collective wisdom growing from sharing stories. If thousands of minds work together, we have a super-brain for hive intelligence to solve the trickiest problems."

"I agree with sharing everything and having a government to run affairs," Bombi said, "but your families love property to excess, which encourages bad motives. To manage a large hyf, you need a vast workforce and organisation to procure, process and protect the goods. That complexity creates anxiety and conflict. Moreover, your bitels take more than they give. Humblebees have chosen a middle ground. We enjoy a more tranquil state of independence with only a few hundred swusters in a family and a modest pantry."

"Hear, hear!" Amma agreed. "We know about their wars between broods and anxiety over the theft of hunig. Those fears are unknown in my tribe and my tiny stenger proves it." She twisted to show her posterior. "I don't need a powerful weapon since I don't own valuables worth stealing. No one threatens me, and I would never hurt or steal from anyone."

Amma deplored all violence. She ridiculed so-called just wars as excuses for aggression that divide societies into winners and losers. She claimed no lifestyle was more peaceable than her own. "You're brainwashed by leaders who need loyal and compliant suckers to keep them in office for building an empire."

Exasperated by the rant, Bombi called her a self-centred insect out of touch with reality and lacking the heart for friendship.

Amma slung back. "I mind my own business, whereas you put your feelers where they aren't wanted. And you are too busy to be playful or have deep thoughts. Life isn't all about work and politics. I can celebrate flowers, kiss baybees and worship Sunne when and wherever I choose. Sometimes, I drop everything I'm doing to marvel at my own existence. I ought to have known better than waste time on bees who have made up their minds, and that's another reason for shunning society."

Bombi tried to end the debate without animosity. She declared all three were happy in their own way and ought to be proud of freely expressing their differences.

They went their own way for the night. Sundew retired to a cranny under the bark of a dead tree, turning over the conversation before falling asleep. Was life any happier in a hermitage than a hive?

Sundew delayed her departure to thank her host. Amma,

not known to be an early riser, crawled out of her den after the sun rose above the trees.

"I thought you had gone," she said. "Have you changed your mind and want this leisurely life instead?"

"You almost convinced me. But last night, I dreamt of nurses caring for baybees and comb-maidens cooking honey. I imagined roaming my hyf to feel weax under my feet, smell our Modor's perfume and meet friends who fret for me. I might die if I don't see Goldenham again.

"I can't imagine being homesick, but you mustn't dally here if you feel like that."

"I'm leaving now but don't know the way home."

"Rubbish. You've got a compass."

Sundew looked as puzzled as if by a new word.

"Listen, I'm no traveller, but I can find my way home if I get lost. The first thing is to relax and clear your head of distracting thoughts. Then, breathe deeply through your spiracles to refresh your body. Don't try to map the route in your head, but allow images, sounds and smells to float up from the unconscious compass in your ganglia. Trust them and appeal to Sunne if they falter."

Sundew listened politely, sure to follow the sun instead of the dotty advice of a mystic. It had delivered her to safety last night, and if the day became too cloudy to see it, she would trust her luck.

Amma's parting words lingered in her mind as she soared away: *Farewell, brave bee. May Sunne bless your journey home to where you belong.*

Desperation to see old friends drove her on, although she knew something precious had been left behind. Amma and Bombi were as different to her and to each other as bees can be, but they showed the kindness of strangers. She remembered her heart glowing as they argued passionately about what they loved most in life. Never before had her own beliefs been so challenged. The encounter felt edgy at times but left her feeling refreshed and more confident. She left her new friends in the sorrow of knowing they would only meet again in memory.

Without a personal guide, Sundew trusted the sun as her navigator. Having only flown before in the early morning or late afternoon, she didn't realize how it moved in a great arc across the sky. Keeping its light in front dazzled her to turn aside from a beeline.

The soft green hills and moist valleys below presented joyful distractions from earnest steering. She had to make corrections to avoid drifting too far south from the sun's course. After making repeated errors, the shepherding sun was too far to her right, and she feared being utterly lost.

An enigmatic impulse then drove her forward, like the wind at your back that knows where it is going. Automatic steering now took over.

Grassy fields changed to crouching shrubs and scattered rocks. The land rose to a heather moor, scarred in places by burnt vegetation. Here and there, a sprinkling of purple blossoms lifted her spirits. The descent from hill country brought renewed determination from the cheer of a pungent sweetness in the air. Sundew's heart leaped at a field of yellow flowers driven by a breeze, like rollers of surf to carry her for the final beat of a homeward journey.

After travelling without a break, she alighted on a flower. A grasshopper lay on its side below, and a weevil nearby. Flying down to examine them, she found more corpses, including a few honeybees. What misadventure befell them that neither predators nor scavengers left them uneaten?

Flickering wings drew attention to a bee still alive and recognized by its stripes. *Skunkie!* She couldn't ignore an appeal for help, even from one of Hemlock's stooges.

"You look sick."

The Hawbrod had fogged eyes and a laboured, croaky voice, "Is that you, Sunnedew? Don't touch the flowers—"

Sundew wouldn't take orders, but then it dawned on her that the warning might have saved her life. "Golly. Has someone poisoned the field? Luckily, I didn't have a drink."

The morbid bee breathed deeply to summon the energy to speak. "I tried to tell Hyacinth about your name . . ." She collapsed before completing the sentence.

"Tell her what?"

"Your plant bad for a maiden flight . . ."

Sundew puzzled over the words to make sense of them. So Skunkie had tried urging them to change her name to something less dangerous than an insectivorous plant. Hemlock chose it to get rid of Sundew if she survived in the vault. And when Skunkie was found out betraying her boss, she paid for it by being sent into the sprayed field.

If Sundew had taken the warning seriously, she might have avoided a dangerous journey and appreciated a secret ally earlier.

"Where you been . . .?" The voice trailed off.

"It's a long story I will tell you later." She said 'later' as a gift of hope and compassion, knowing it lied to a dying insect.

Skunkie slumped, her legs unable to support her weight any longer. She mumbled: "Go quickly and save the hyf."

CHAPTER 15
Surprise in the Spinney

A wake of bees followed Joe as he trundled a box of honeycomb in a barrow across the meadow. He thought they tagged after him for humming like the Pied Piper. More likely, they smelled honey.

Cuthbert waited at the shed, amazed at Joe's bravado in only a T-shirt and shorts. That boy didn't do things by halves and wanted to prove that he was all-in with beekeeping. Neither of the monks told his mother the outfit she made never left its peg. Nor did they mention to their brothers they had a new star in the bee-yard to avoid the abbot hearing.

"Looks like another bumper harvest," Cuthbert said. "The bees will be glad of peace when it's over."

Brother Adam came out to test the weight of the box before Cuthbert wheeled it away to the refectory. Other monks would fill jars with honey spun from frames in an extractor.

"I'm surprised you can lift it, boy," he mumbled.

"How many jars of honey does that make?" Joe asked.

"Up to forty from each box."

Whistling from a quick calculation, Joe reckoned the shop would make a few thousand pounds in sales. His new hive might earn serious pocket money next year. He slipped inside the shed to bring it out.

"What are you doing? It should stay inside until next spring when I give you a colony."

"I want to attract a swarm for free."

"Bah! Not this late in the season. Don't come crying if vermin spoil it."

Joe didn't like to be told what to do with his handiwork. He had already lost an argument over the design of his starter hive. The monk contended he should be satisfied with eight 'medium' frames per box instead of ten 'deeps'. Joe wanted the larger container for more honey.

"Don't forget to tidy up before you go."

He didn't take so much offence now at a man too old to change his ways. As Adam tottered to the abbey, he rested the hive on blocks a short distance from the shed.

Ambling along the path, Joe was alert for wildlife and swung loose arms that held a butterfly net until the week before. He delighted in an acrobatic peewit calling its own name, a hedgehog nosing for beetles in a dung pile, and a dragonfly darting like an arrow. He decided to ask his mum for a pair of binoculars instead of a new bike for his birthday.

A faint haze across the field hung over the spinney, and the breeze brought a whiff of wood smoke. Had someone lit a fire in his camp?

The crackle of dry leaves and twigs underfoot made a stealthy approach to the camp impossible. Nevertheless, Joe crouched to be sure the clearing was empty. Nothing stirred except a column of smoke rising from glowing sticks that someone had arranged like wheel spokes. Whoever discovered his hideout couldn't have gone far. Perhaps a tramp lit the fire and left to check rabbit snares. Joe might see the vagabond in the field or snoop on him from aloft in the treehouse if he came back to cook a meal.

The first stage of the climb was the trickiest. He had to leap on a dangling rope, using monkey legs to cling on and swinging to grab the lowest bough. He hardly noticed rustling in the bushes before pounding feet came up behind. Rough hands tugged his legs off the rope to make him fall with outstretched hands to absorb the impact of hitting the dirt.

Before he could roll over, a knee in his back pinned him to the ground and took the wind out of his lungs. Then, his arms were twisted back for binding with a slipknot around the wrists. The ruffian's heavy body subdued Joe's resistance for tying ankles together and yanking them over his bum to secure to his wrists.

Lying hog-tied on his belly, he couldn't move his arms or legs. Struggling made the bonds bite deeper. He hollered words never uttered at home except the day his dad accidentally slammed a car door on a finger.

In a flashback to last year, he remembered an interview on TV with a solemn policeman appealing for help with inquiries about a Devonshire boy who had gone missing. He also mentioned another kidnap victim the police had never found alive. Although the cases happened on the far side of the county, mothers waited at the school gate in the afternoons for months after the broadcast instead of letting their kids walk home. Joe's mum baked a rich fruitcake usually reserved for his birthday. She would be heartbroken to lose her only child. He vowed to be a better son if God let him go free to hug her again.

The agony of not knowing his fate ended when a boot hooked under his belly to flip him over. He stared at the villain's face. "Brad!"

A quick answer to prayer gave him massive relief. The bigger boy would untie him after giving him a scare, so the day would end well.

"Yer look like a suckling pig for roasting!" Brad gloated over his prey. His shiner had changed to greengage from mulberry that matched the colour of Brad's dyed hair. He tossed greenery on the fire and dragged Joe closer to make him cough. Smoke watered his eyes.

Brad regarded him with the indifference of a cow chewing the cud. He blew a bubble of gum and sucked it back to pound between molar teeth. Joe closed his eyes, knowing a score was being settled. Although Brad missed his target, Joe felt a rain of spittle on his face.

"Still like playing soldiers, Ginge?" Brad chuckled. "It ain't no fun to be a prisoner in yer own camp."

Joe avoided firing back to avoid prolonging the torture until his captor had satisfied revenge. The bully always interviewed insubordinate gang members by pulling heads back by the hair.

"Yer can't 'ide from me, not behind a girl's skirt or on yer mother's lap."

"I don't want any trouble." Joe replied, hot and sweaty.

"The trouble is the monkeys took the box my grandpa found. Finders are keepers. Promise to get it and I'll forget the favour I'm owed."

So he didn't harass Joe as payback for thinking Joe deliberately deceived him about the monk's bottle. Instead, Brad wanted a box—that box!

Joe blamed his cousin for dragging him into an obsessive quest. Perhaps the gang had heard her blabbing in the village or had spied on them going to the tomb. But why did he ask for help after the monk locked the tomb? He needed a locksmith instead of Joe!

"I can't get it since they locked the mouseoleum," Joe blurted out, hoping to end the suffering.

"The what—?" Brad laughed out loud when he understood. "They aren't so stupid to keep it there. It's in that 'ive behind the shed. Bees are better guards than locks for keeping nosy people away."

Swearing he had seen the box on the abbot's tomb got Joe's hair twisted by a few more degrees.

"Don't lie to me, kiddo. The ole monkey in the nursing 'ome told my mum they keep it in the bottom of that 'ive."

Joe suddenly felt unsure of what he had seen in the gloom. Emily had imagined a treasure chest, but he recalled a small oblong box with a narrow slit at one end. A slit!

That rang a bell. He had seen a similar box in the shed. The monk called it a 'nuc' box for keeping the nucleus of a new colony before installing bees in a proper hive. Did he leave the box on the slab in tribute to the old abbot? Joe never trusted Brad, but why would he make it up? Having never seen inside the bottom box, he regretted not asking.

"What's so special about a box? You should ask the monk."

"The crazy old geezer won't give it up."

"I can make you a nicer hive box," Joe said. He pretended to be ignorant because Brad hadn't mentioned treasure, possibly worried if Joe would take it for himself.

"Don't be a prat. It's another box inside the 'ive and easy-peasy for a beekeeper to get."

Brad's agitated manner showed there must be something valuable at stake. Frustrated by the lack of cooperation, he tugged a cord to make Joe squeal, then paced up and down, looking unsure what to do.

Meanwhile, Joe pieced together what he knew. Emily was onto something, although her pet theory was wrong. His mind whirled to think of Adam keeping the secret for donkey's years until Baldred spilt the beans to Norma Grattich after losing his wits. The Grattiches needed to bully a beekeeper into opening the hive they wouldn't dare do.

Joe could get the box while the monks were at prayers.

However, the consequences of getting caught would be more severe than pinching a few apples or a bottle. Sooner or later, the monk would find the bottom of the hive empty, or an advertisement would draw notice to a sale of rare antiquities. The sweetness of getting the gang leader off his back would then turn sour. As an accessory to theft, the publicity would disgrace his family and make him a pariah in the village. Better to face a beating now for peace in the future.

A boot in the loins took his breath away and he lowered his eyes, expecting another blow. But Brad stepped away to prepare a nuclear solution. He dug in his leather jacket pocket and pulled out a red tube, the same kind he laid on the gate post.

"Maybe this will convince yer," he said grimly and flashed it under Joe's nose. He was subtle by not revealing if the end was open or had a dimple in the brass cap at the other end. Either would prove it had been fired.

Joe didn't flinch at a wild threat from a boy too young for a gun licence. He shook his head. Brad could be brutal scrapping with boys on the playground who came away with bloody noses. Still, he wouldn't threaten someone with live ammo, would he? And yet, a gamekeeper's son could take a live shell from his father's cartridge belt as deftly as nicking a cigarette from a pack of Woodbines.

"Why so stubborn when it's no skin off yer nose? The monkeys don't care about the box in the 'hive or they wouldn't keep it there. This is yer last chance to go 'ome in one piece."

Joe had cramps from sitting in bonds for a half-hour and was getting desperate to be released. But he gambolled that refusing to cooperate would triumph. So he felt nervous when more kindling was tossed on the fire. Brad danced around like a demon, warbling a ludicrous ditty:

> *Holy Joe sits coughing in the smoke,*
> *Waiting for a bang to make 'im croak.*

He was a lousy actor, possibly put up to it by the same person who gave him a black eye. He waved the shell in the air before laying it a few inches from glowing sticks.

Joe scrunched his eyes to drain salty water for focussing on the shell. He strained to see the direction it pointed. As Brad backed away, Joe thought he looked a little sorry for his captive, not something he ever saw in that boy before. Joe yelled until Brad was out of sight.

He hadn't feared an explosion while his tormentor remained, but now alone his imagination flared. The sticks burned like a slow fuse towards a shell he assumed to be dead but couldn't be certain. Who knew what happened when ammunition gets hot? Does it spray lead shot as out of a barrel or harmlessly go phut? People in the lane hearing a loud bang out of the hunting season might assume a car backfired. He could lie there bleeding for hours until rescue came.

Most likely, Brad would come back soon to savour the fright he gave him and throw an empty shell away. He would untie Joe and laugh if he had soiled his pants.

Brad could deny being there: one boy's word against another. Besides, Joe had disadvantages. He had a record of lighting outdoor fires, and his parents once found him playing with a live shell dropped by a careless toff from the pheasant shoot. It was unjust if Brad got away with bullying, but there would be consequences from exposing his delinquency.

Alone in the wood, Joe began to panic as much about the bonds as the shell. They might permanently harm hands or feet already numb from cutting off the blood supply like a tourniquet. Straining for the folded knife in the back pocket he sat on, he rubbed against something sharp in the dirt and then felt a warm trickle on his wrist.

CHAPTER 16
The Wanderer Returns

Every hero deserves a triumphant homecoming. Sundew planned to take a lap around the hive to surprise the family. Field bees would convey the news for Sage to record her adventures for posterity. But Skunkie knew something about the hive that required a cautious approach.

Instead of bustling with traffic, the entrance looked abnormally quiet. A pungent chemical odour replaced the soothing perfume of its resident queen.

The dread of loneliness crept back; so weird to feel in the least expected place. Did the family die of a plague or flee from an attack? Sundew hovered near the entrance, hoping a caretaker stayed behind with their new address. The thrill of a head emerging from the slit vanished at the last face in the world she wanted to see. It wasn't, however, the self-confident countenance from before her maiden flight.

"Hemlock!" She deliberately used a nickname instead of a formal title. "I might have guessed you would still be here. Tell me where they went, and don't lie."

Sundew overcame the shock faster than Hemlock, who

stared back too stunned to notice she had been called by an insulting nickname. Something had changed.

"Holy frass! Are you Sunnedew's ghost?"

"I'm no ghost. Tell me if Cwen Goldenrod is safe."

"Only Sunne knows."

"Don't try to trick me again."

"Who knows where a swarm goes? A four-legs left a stink under the hyf that made us too sick to work. Your brod didn't have the guts to stay and took all the honey they could carry."

"Huh! So you finally got your wish to take over the hyf. Who gave you such a black heart to be in league with a wicked four-legs?"

"We would never help anyone harming our beloved home. Don't you think we have suffered enough from losing our cwen and unable to make baybees? Have a care for our history instead of listening to tales of your brave colonists taking over."

Having heard Hemlock telling whoppers before, Sundew didn't trust her now. Nevertheless, she listened to grudges pouring out like water from a burst dam.

"Hawbrods were the strongest family in the meadow. We had full boxes of hunig and baybees, yet no one dared to rob us. But after Goldenrod replaced our cwen, her swusters took all the credit for building our mansion and prosperity. Imagine how it feels to be downgraded to a second-class citizen in your own home. How would you feel if foreigners took yours over?"

The passion on her face showed a sincere belief in her complaints. Still, Sundew refused to be moved without hearing remorse for past brutalities.

"Perhaps we aren't as far apart as you think," Hemlock continued. "I am a lonely orphan, and you grieve for your cwen. There is no food in the pantry, and your swusters may starve from going feral. We have all lost out. See if you can find your family, but I will stay here to make this a sweet home again. Perhaps the nursery will have baybee Hawbrods again. One of our workers felt her ovaries growing since your cwen's scent no longer suppresses our fertility."

"I thought workers who lay eggs can only make broders."

"If so, we will ask our cousins in the lower hyfs to send a spare cwen."

The Hawbrods were clutching at broken straws. They couldn't restore a balanced family by breeding male drones alone. A substitute queen might be rejected by workers even if related to them.

Sundew entered the hive to avoid listening to more whining. The stench almost drove her out again. It rose through the wire mesh under her feet that the keeper fitted for ventilating the hive. She clambered to the nursery on the next storey, where doting nurses used to care for wriggling larvae. Those cells now lay empty. After breathing the toxic vapour, the remaining staff staggered around with gormless faces. Seeing the nursey desolate, there seemed no point in looking further: nothing is more calamitous than losing the seedbed of future generations.

Before exiting, she felt the woodwork shudder. Earthquakes didn't happen in that district, and the keeper never jolted the hive during an inspection. She found Hemlock outside counselling a group of sisters with drawn faces.

"Now, do you believe me?" Hemlock looked grey. "We thought the monster left for good after leaving a stink, but it came back. Feel the tremors as frames are torn out of the top storey. These old fighters are ready for action, even if doomed for failure. There's nothing to keep you here, but tell Sage a story of valiant defenders who refused to surrender while any remain alive."

Sundew took off to watch events from overhead. Hemlock commanded her veterans and a few younger flyers led by Shady to form squadrons. They zoomed into formation to attack the monster. It leaned over the hive, frantically tugging at frames stuck together with bee glue. It batted the bees away as they closed in, but they circled for another attempt. Those getting through a barrage of waving limbs were squashed before they could sting.

As Sundew observed the battle, she wondered if the phantasmagoric Mangeapis had come back. This monster looked different from the image she had from Sage, but descriptions passed through generations of storytellers get distorted or embellished. One day, she hoped to tell her family what the monster really looked like.

Instead of a black-and-white striped head and furry body, it had a thicket of brown hair on its head and a floppy blue skin covering its legs and middle. Contrary to its reputation for an insatiable appetite, it didn't eat the honey spilled from broken frames. And, strangest of all, a short white stick poked out of its mouth, glowing at the tip. Sundew wondered what kind of craziness triggered the wicked spree.

She had a new respect for the Hawbrods from their brave defence. Setting aside past antagonism, she admitted they were cousins and shared a birthplace. Allegiance to different queens made them enemies, which Amma would think absurd. Although harder to revise an opinion about Hemlock, she admired the commander for sharing the risks of combat with her brood.

Sundew flew down to join Hemlock orbiting the aggressor's head to find a target of soft, pink skin between bushy hair.

"I thought you had left, Sunnedew," she said when their circuits crossed.

"It's painful to watch this unequal fight. I can't be a bystander while a common enemy destroys our home. I want to join the fight if you let bygones be bygones."

Hemlock looked incredulously at the giant bee she had persecuted and opposed in the brood war. Yet, Sundew showed sincerity in her eyes, not for friendship but the gift of unity in desperate times.

The raider had ransacked four boxes, leaving only two intact, and was intent on finishing the destruction. Sundew proposed a new tactic: if Hemlock feigned an attack to distract attention, she would make the strike before it noticed. Hemlock agreed on the condition that she had the first chance to stab the enemy.

They prepared for action while the veterans continued their futile sorties below. When the monster struggled to separate frames in Box 2, Sundew bore down on it, but too slowly. A limb lashing out sent her crashing to the ground. After a blow that made her see stars, she came out of a stupor to hear a familiar voice.

"Are you okay? Please say something."

With a clearer head, she saw Hemlock leaning over her.

"Phew. I stopped the attack to check if you were a goner. Luckily you only got bruised on your back."

Sundew didn't reply. To call it a mite bite would remind her new ally that she sent her to the Cryptum.

They repeated the plan, except this time Sundew kept a safer distance and buzzed loudly to draw the monster's notice. Hemlock darted at an island of bare skin and squeezed her poison gland as hard as possible. She couldn't drag the sting out afterwards. The monster made a vulgar cry as it dropped the stick from its mouth and brushed her off with a claw.

Sundew watched Hemlock fall. She had fought deadly duels with wasps and seen casualties in wartime but never witnessed the violent death of a comrade. To see a known life snuffed out in a flash shook her to the core. The limp body in the grass left mingling feelings of admiration and sorrow. She felt none of the relief of seeing a deceased wasp because Hemlock had joined the legendary company of warrior bees.

A partnership severed by the death of an ally released her from the obligation to continue the fight. She was free to leave veterans to tackle the angry monster now making a ferocious assault on Box 2. Who could prevail against such a titanic force? Why make a sacrifice if all were doomed and the only witness a mute sun?

She circled the field, intending to leave but halting every time at the boundary. Nowhere was far enough to erase the memory of a dear home. The upper meadow would be impoverished without the stack of painted boxes beloved by generations of bees. The keepers had a stake, too, and more than as just a trading station. They relaxed in the yard to chat and hum to its residents.

Sundew had seen wondrous places in her travels but never a lovelier place or yearned to live anywhere except at home. To forsake the hive would fail a duty her former arch-enemy understood. If the family came back to build a home, Sage might expunge her from their history for desertion at a critical moment.

Unless she stopped dithering, she might live with regret. The sight of the Mangeapis kicking the bottom boxes tipped her from passive anger into a fit of blazing fury. But she needed another tactic to confront a determined foe.

The wise queen never named in the myth didn't make a frontal assault on the monster. Instead, she found a tender place on its head beside a lobe of wrinkly skin. It didn't see her coming from the side because monsters can't see all around as bees can.

Sundew dived into the pit and squeezed through the short passage. It smelled rancid and felt greasy, nothing like fresh beeswax. She stabbed the membranous end wall once for every broken frame until her poison ran dry, and safely withdrew the sting. Had Hemlock owned a similar repeater, she might still be alive.

The monster's scream conducted through skull bones sounded even louder to her than to bees outside. The monster shook its head violently to dislodge her from the waxy 'cell', and failing that, it tried winkling her out with a claw too fat to enter.

Her chance to escape came with a new sensation of being jogged up and down. Tempted to peer out, she saw the scenery sweeping past as the monster galloped across the meadow on its hind legs. She launched from the lobe, relieved to put the howling noise behind her.

After saving the remains of the hive, she hoped the keepers could restore the rest to make a home for another brood. She made a final flypast before leaving to search for her family.

Seeing a small hive near the shed, she swooped to investigate the closest refuge to home. The boxes smelling of new wood were empty apart from bare sheets of wax foundation. How odd that keepers would leave a vacant property for vagrants to take over.

Heading to the garden, she met pollinators flitting to their favourite colours and flavours. It brought back memories of her first flight with Daisy. The lavender bed attracted a host of feeders to a glut of nectar, but no one knew where her swarm had gone.

All the bees had the tan stripes of the grey hives, except one individual flashing past with the brown stripes of her brood. Struggling to keep up with the relative, she was relieved when it halted at the abbey wall and slowly traced the joints between stone blocks. Tailing it to the gutter, she watched it crawl into the shadow of a downpipe and re-emerge. The bee was so self-absorbed that she supposed it had gone bonkers from breathing poison in the hive. On turning back to the garden, she heard a voice calling her.

"Bless my spiracles, is that you, Sunnedew? I never thought we'd see you again." The bee looked flabbergasted. "Do you remember me? I'm Marigold, a cell capper in your box? After we swarmed, they appointed me to scout for a new home."

"I'm thrilled to see you after finding the hyf empty except for a few Hawbrods. I hung around for a while to help them defend it from a monster who was tearing it apart."

"Hmm. I'm surprised you allied with them. They ridiculed us for leaving after Sage had a premonition of worse to come than the great stink."

She told Sundew the swarm had made a temporary camp in a tree while waiting for scouts to bring proposals for a permanent home. After a fruitless search of the garden, Marigold looked for crevices in the abbey wall. Finding a gap under the eaves that opened to roof space, she didn't need to look further for a secure place close to a prime dining area.

After skipping breakfast, the scout needed a snack before the pair headed for the swarm. As they crossed a barren lawn to inspect the menu on the flower borders, the irresistible whiff of honey kindled appetites for the supreme meal. They traced it to a bowl on a table where keepers sat with friends.

The party gave only mild resistance to them buzzing around, so they landed to gorge at the edge of the golden pool. An arm revolving over the table disturbed them before they finished, but they didn't go far. When Marigold returned first, she buzzed in frustration at the covered bowl. The only accessible honey was coating a pink claw held up to tempt them. Sundew alighted on it, unable to resist the liquor and sure it wouldn't harm her.

"Be careful, or it may eat you!" Marigold yelled in agitation.

Feeling a jolt, Sundew decided not to linger. She joined the scout on a direct route to the swarm. In their rear vision, they saw the junior keeper lurching off the bench to follow them.

CHAPTER 17
Chasing a Beeline

The figure curled on the garden bench looked as dozy as the dormouse at the Hatter's tea party. The youngsters sat quietly on the other side of the table. Emily checked her wristwatch and whispered, "It's too early to wake him."

Brother Adam rolled over and rubbed his eyes. The cousins expected him to bawl at them, but he said mildly, "I needed forty winks before your party. Let's cross fingers that my brother remembers the *pièce de résistance*."

Smacking his lips betrayed a weakness for dessert, so contrary to his stony disposition. He concealed the surprise in French words, although they had seen Mrs. B baking a sponge for Cuthbert to finish.

Cuthbert plodded across the lawn with a loaded tray. "Not a blemish in the sky today," he said, "except for Emily's cloud preparing to scud off to London. I thought she preferred this life to noise and smoke in the city." He grinned at his brother. "We talked about her going into a rural nunnery after leaving school."

They all knew it was farthest from her ambitions, and she couldn't help blushing cheeks.

"Without your help, it will be hard to control your cousin's new enthusiasm for bees," Cuthbert continued. "Not everyone hearing about his talent will appreciate it." Adam absorbed a thin smile, probably brooding over the future of his bee-yard.

"He needs to be taken down a peg or two," Emily said. "A novice beekeeper should be stung at least once for the bees to remind him he isn't a hive boss."

Joe grimaced at the gentle mockery that Cuthbert compounded.

"If he wants them to pay him homage as a king bee, Mrs. B should make him a suit with big brown stripes and angel wings."

Adam ended the frivolity by pointing at the bandage around Joe's wrist. Joe whisked his hand under the table, wishing he wore long sleeves as he had already endured interrogation at home.

"Did your mother dress the wound with honey? It's the best antiseptic." The old monk never missed an opportunity to extol hive products.

"He told us he fell over a fence," Emily chipped in. "I think he's too nimble for that accident and barbs make puncture wounds instead of a gash."

He refused to be drawn even as all eyes turned to him.

Keeping his mouth shut wasn't stoical; it was sensible not to give adults reasons to stir up trouble. He decided to act as if nothing had happened in the spinney the next time he met Brad. You can't antagonise an enemy likely to be met in a tiny village.

The youngsters debated in advance what they would say if the monks discussed the apparent break-in at the mausoleum. Fortunately, the brothers didn't.

Emily still nursed a frustration with the locked door that had killed her story. And Joe couldn't disclose the box in the tomb was a red herring or she would want to know how he learned about the monk's wilier hiding place. It would make Emily mad to think how close they came every time they attended an inspection. And if she knew, she might put pressure on him to look in the hive.

The week ahead promised less drama without her around or Brad to worry about. Boredom never seemed attractive before.

Cuthbert returned to the refectory for a kettle of water to brew tea while Emily left the table to view the borders for the last time. The mix of flowers changed with the season, now dominated by chrysanthemums as portents of autumn. The monk leaned over to Joe. "Bring me a jar for her to take home."

Joe scooted off, glad to be trusted alone in the shed. After nosing around, he spied a row of paint cans on a shelf above Emily's bee suit. They reminded him to paint ravens on his hive.

Standing on a chair, he grasped a can with a black slick down its side and prised off the lid with his blade. Stabbing the rubbery skin confirmed it contained liquid paint underneath. Wobbling on the chair, he reached with one hand to steady himself against the wall but tipped the can over to make an ugly black streak down the front of the suit.

After frantically hunting for a solvent, he found a bottle of turpentine to slosh over the stain and rub with a rag. It left a smudge and heavy vapour. Thankfully, the old man had lost his sense of smell, so he might get away without Brother Adam noticing.

He snatched a jar from the cupboard to hurry back to the party. Looking back from the gate, he checked the shed door was shut. He hadn't noticed before a frame lying on the grass, so he ran to the far side of the shed to see if the hive was alright.

A scene of devastation brought him to a standstill. Where a stack of six boxes once stood, only two remained intact. The other four lay on their sides with frames scattered higgledy-piggledy. A hurricane can knock a hive over, but the weather had been calm. Rogue badgers are raiders, but they never leave honeycomb uneaten. Apart from the violent damage, the scene was uncannily calm. Joe expected insects to be storming around their ruined home, but only a couple flew in monotonous circles.

He rushed back and plonked the jar on the table, making his mum gripe about running with glass in his hand. It was hard to find words to describe the scene.

"Hmm. Hmm. Someone smashed your hive, sir . . ."

Heads around the table turned to each other and then to him. His earnest face proved he wasn't kidding.

Adam followed him to the meadow as fast as his creaky joints allowed. He threw up his arms at seeing the wreckage and stumbled across the turf, making woeful sounds. Casting eyes over it for a long time, his face turned as pure white as his hair. While trying to comprehend the scene, the gate clicked to announce Emily's arrival.

"Joe! Is it true? Your mum has arrived and wants to know what's keeping you."

She put a hand over her mouth when she saw Joe bending over the ruins to save the least damaged frames.

"Who would do such a thing?"

"It's worse than it looks. Someone stole the bees."

A package of ordinary bees is worth a few pounds, but no one could put a price on prize bees. Their value was inestimable until the queen bred enough daughters for others to appraise. Beekeepers want more productive honeybees as farmers are eager for leaner pigs, milkier cows and fleecier sheep. In his heyday, the monk had won fame for creating the Oldburgh stock that spread across the globe. He kept his latest project to himself, not for fear of being stolen but of ridicule for an impossible ambition in his dotage.

Emily asked if a dishonest beekeeper had stolen the brood. Who else had a motive or the mettle? Joe shook his head. A keeper with any sense would block the hive entrance and cart all the boxes away intact. But unfortunately, he didn't have another explanation.

The youngsters avoided more questions or eye contact out of respect for his grief. Emily ran back to convey news to Cuthbert and Mrs. B while the boy helped the monk to reassemble a hive reduced to five boxes.

Seeing a white ball in the grass the size of a marble, Joe got down on his hands and knees to pocket it. He found many more under the hive, and the smell on his hands made him screw up his nose. The monk's face darkened when presented with them in the boy's cupped palm.

"I think they're mothballs, sir." He remembered how his mother's wardrobe reeked.

"They are toxic, so don't put fingers in your mouth until you've washed your hands."

"Do mothballs make bees go away the same as clothes moths?"

A flinty look confirmed it, but the monk couldn't frame the theory settling in Joe's mind. He guessed Brad used them to drive the insects away. That explained everything except the failure to break into the bottom box, still glued to the one above. If Brad was disturbed during the raid, he would certainly return at a quiet time for the treasure.

Whatever the youngsters thought of the prickly monk before, he had their sympathy now. After the fire on the moor, he had vested his most precious hope in the one queen. Now she had flown and taken a swarm with her.

Cuthbert struggled to comfort him while others listened with long faces. "It's heart-breaking, Brother. We understand if you want to cancel the party and be alone in your cell."

The old monk didn't look up from his lap. The garden rarely hosted a more sombre gathering, even after a funeral. Cuthbert prayed for the bees before pouring tea that had turned cold from stewing in the pot. The group munched bread and honey in silence. Even the prospect of strawberry gateau failed to raise their spirits.

Cuthbert cleared his throat to alert them to unexpected visitors. "Ahem. Someone heard about our dessert."

Abbot Godwin strolled up with a postulant slightly older than Emily. Still looking in a blue funk, Adam kept his head down while Cuthbert told their superior about the crime. He asked if they should report it to the police.

"Don't bother the busy constable. It is a shame if a vandal came on our grounds, although he may have done us a favour. We have more hives than we can cope with."

Cuthbert concealed whatever he thought of the careless remark. Perhaps he gave the abbot the benefit of the doubt for not knowing how close Adam came to a splendid achievement. He tried to revive spirits by complimenting the youngsters.

"May I introduce Mrs. B's niece, Father Abbot? Emily is as sharp as a tack and will be a famous writer. And we should call her young cousin the hive hummer of Oldburgh." He gave Joe a sly smile.

"I'll see you both at Vespers," the abbot said and turned to Mrs. Brawson. "Pity we don't see your boy more often at our services."

When the visitors left, Cuthbert pressed his palms together to declare, "Let's celebrate the holy mystery of Mrs. B's baking." He winked at her, and she gave him a coy grin back. "I topped the sponge with double cream and fresh strawberries from flowers kissed by my brother's bees."

The attempt to bring life to the party produced strained smiles. Adam didn't look at his slice of gateau but had a changed manner. He had a new gleam in his eyes, and the furrows on his brow had rolled smooth.

"Nobody stole my bees," he said, looking up. "They won't be far away if they swarmed to avoid an acrid smell. They are probably sending out scouts to choose a new home. We can track their beelines."

He had to explain to puzzled faces. "Tribal people hunting for honeycomb can follow wild bees back to their nests because they fly in straight lines to save energy. A scout bee can lead us to the swarm."

Joe chuckled to imagine the monks chasing a bee across the countryside, one old and skinny and the other jolly and tubby. What was he thinking? Even Cuthbert sounded doubtful.

"It's a topping idea, Brother, but let's have the gateau first."

Adam made a sigh of exasperation, easy for him to leave the table with no appetite. Moments later, Mrs. Brawson laid down her fork to swish bees away from the honey bowl.

"We should've checked if they are scouts," Joe said, wiping cream from his lips on a bandaged wrist.

"They probably came from the grey hives. What do you think, Brother?" Cuthbert forked a large strawberry in his mouth.

Adam dipped a finger in the honey and covered the bowl with a saucer to prevent the bees from feeding there. Everyone knew the act and they didn't wait long until the bait tempted one. He strained through his spectacles to focus on it perched on his fingertip.

"Come here, boy. You have sharper eyes."

Joe scrambled to look over his shoulder. "It's a big bee without stripes, maybe a queen."

"Yes, yes, it's a queen, but is there a yellow dot on its back? I marked the Peacemaker after rescuing her from the moor."

"I can't see a dot," he replied and paused for a moment's silence before giving an explosive shriek. "Crikey! We've seen it before. You must look, Emmy. It's the bee we saved from the sundew in the bog."

His clumsy move jolted the arm holding the bee. It flew off in alarm to deny others a chance to examine it.

"It can't be the same. The dustmen took the jar away to the dump." She glanced at her aunt to see if the remark embarrassed her.

Joe refused to back down. "I saw a red scar on its back and bet there isn't another like it in the world. I'm going to catch it."

He leapt off the bench, ignoring his mother nagging him to finish his tea. No one took him seriously. They thought him mad to track a single bee across a garden full of hummers, although Emily cheered, and the monk gave him a nod. Cuthbert bit his lip as the boy trampled across the flower bed to sprint out of sight into the field.

Joe returned thirty minutes later with a red face and hair more ruffled than usual. His mum pointed to his plate. "Sit down and apologise to Brother Cuthbert before finishing your dessert."

Joe didn't stop talking between scoops of strawberries and cream, and no one paid closer attention than the old monk. "They were too fast, so I kept going straight across the fields where a swarm has nowhere to rest. I had to stop at a fence because frisky cattle guarded the other side—"

"Get to the point, boy. Did you or didn't you see a swarm? There's no mistaking it." The suspense was killing the monk, who didn't want details of the caper if it ended in disappointment.

"I couldn't shoo them away from under a huge chestnut tree, but bees kept coming and going from there."

The monk chuckled and held up a V-sign, like Winston Churchill.

Joe jogged back to the tree on the main path, followed

by Emily carrying a folded cardboard box and the monk at the rear. The tree could grace a landscape painting. Green prickly capsules containing conkers hung in dense palms of foliage casting a circle of shade over dried mud imprinted by hooves.

Seeing the trio, the cattle left the shade with lowered heads as if relishing a chase to relieve a dull day. Joe reckoned he could beat them to the tree in a ten-second dash, rather optimistically for a stretch of one hundred yards. The monk reminded him that people are killed every year by stampeding livestock in the English countryside.

One of the beasts trotted to the fence nodding in a pretence of friendship. Joe suggested they stare it down as Mowgli drove off the tiger Shere Khan. The monk scoffed at the idea. Instead, he asked Emily to lure the herd away by making a hullabaloo along the fence line until they were out of sight. Others will follow where one inquisitive beast goes.

Sorry to miss the action, Emily left waving her arms to attract the cattle's attention and sang *"Proud to be a Cow"*, filling forgotten lines from *Sesame Street* with *"la-la-la"*. As soon as the monk signalled an all-clear, Joe led him across the gap at a leisurely pace.

A murmur of humming drew them to the swarm, a

brown globe hanging from a bough like a rugby ball. Its surface writhed with workers protecting their queen deep in the core. The monk leaned back to gaze at the lost colony.

Until the box unfolded, Joe had been too absorbed in discovery to wonder how they would get the swarm down. Once the box was laid underneath, it came as a jolt for him to realise the monk's plan, which was scarier than his introduction to bees. A successful outcome depended on him, for who else could do the climbing?

Would his gift for calming bees around hives still work when tens of thousands were unemployed outside? He would be as vulnerable in the chestnut tree as the day monks caught him in the orchard. And jumping to escape from bees from twenty feet up might break a leg. Even a vindictive abbot wouldn't wish that on him.

The monk tapped his shoulder. "Ready to go? There's no need to worry about them because they don't have any honeycomb to protect."

Easy for him to say. Joe felt like an army conscript waiting in the trenches for the order to engage well-armed adversaries.

"Be prepared if they fly out when disturbed," the monk continued. "Obey the rule to stay calm, so they don't think you threaten them. I'm more worried about you falling, though I understand you are an expert climber."

The old man bent over and braced himself with hands against the tree's bole for the boy to climb on his back to reach the first bough. Joe found easy footholds from there to the horizontal limb where the swarm dangled on a thin branch. He crept along until directly overhead to check the drop like a bomber taking aim at a ground target. The box needed to move slightly for greater accuracy. He would revel at giving orders to the monk in other circumstances but had to steel himself now.

The ball of insects shuddered as he sawed the branch with a blade from his Swiss army knife. Guards flew out to check the disturbance. Watching the drama above, the monk suggested he try humming, but Joe was too frozen to make a sound. When the insects settled again, the monk advised sawing with even strokes to fool them into thinking they swayed in a breeze.

As the branch thinned to a strand, Joe wondered what would happen when the ball hit the ground. No lesson prepared him for the detonation of vengeful insects.

The branch snapped, taking him by surprise. He jerked back too quickly to see it fall but heard a splat. The manila cardboard vanished under a shroud of brown insects.

Hands clapping below confirmed it fell on target.

He returned to the tree trunk and sprung as confident as a monkey to the lowest bough. But before jumping off, he overlooked roots exposed by ground erosion.

Emily yelled from across the fence as he lay on his back, grasping his leg and moaning. By the time she arrived, the monk was sitting with an arm over the boy's shoulder. "You did it. You did it, Joe! The Peacemakers are in the box."

Emily removed his shoe to feel bones in his foot. "Does this hurt? Is it numb?" She suspected he had sprained his ankle.

They sat with backs to the trunk to watch a spectacle. After getting over their alarm, flyers landed among others marching in a contracting circle to join teeming numbers inside the box. The queen's scent attracted them like iron filings to a magnet. When most had disappeared inside, the monk flipped the flaps over and sealed gaps with tape. Those that didn't make it in time had to find their way by scent.

An afternoon that began with a sedate tea party switched to a crime scene and then a rescue mission. After riding roller-coaster emotions, the trio congratulated each other for working together to save the swarm. But Joe had some qualms he couldn't hide. He warned that the person who poisoned the hive might strike again. And he urged the monk to transfer it closer to the abbey for greater security but was told the abbot would forbid it.

"Why not house them in my hive instead? Perhaps the vandal chose the painted one for a reason and might ignore mine." Of course, he couldn't say more without exposing himself to questions about how he came by that knowledge.

The monk replied that Joe's hive was too small and the bees would be happier in familiar boxes after the bad air cleared.

Joe felt annoyed by the intransigence and having advice blown off. The monk thought it was a random attack never to be repeated. Besides, he probably wanted to keep the treasure box with a bee colony to defend it. The little hive couldn't accommodate both.

Apart from that minor spat, nothing spoiled a triumphant return. Emily carried the box ahead of Joe, who hobbled beside the monk to the garden. His mum had already left to open the shop, leaving Cuthbert to guard the table. He winked at Joe from behind an empty platter.

"Sorry! I couldn't let your mum's sponge go soggy."

CHAPTER 18
The Phoney Peace

Sundew flew ahead of Marigold when she saw the ball of insects hanging from a tree bough. She expected a rapturous welcome from the family after an absence of several days. So she felt bitterly disappointed when nobody greeted her except a sniffy guard who checked her scent as a passport to allow her inside.

Marigold hustled her through the multitude. "Hurry, or I'll be late for the general assembly. I mustn't miss my chance to present plans for a future home and am counting on your vote for the stone hive."

The proceedings had already begun when they joined a packed audience listening to the first scout. She recommended making a nest in a hollow tree at the edge of a wood. The idea appealed to bees with romantic notions of a traditional home and those wanting to be independent of keepers. However, some listeners objected that although it might look homely, a fixed space would force the family to split when they outgrew it. Those moving out would have to search for a home all over again.

Sundew loathed a proposal that divided a family. She

thought the vacant hive near the shed was superior and could be expanded to accommodate a large population. Marigold cautioned that only certified scouts were allowed to offer proposals at the assembly.

The proceedings suddenly halted as the ball of insects swayed on the twig. Only the crush of bodies against each other prevented them from falling over.

"Don't panic. It's only the wind and nothing to worry about," an official assured them.

The first scout concluded with a dance to express confidence in her proposal. Marigold sneered that she would dance with greater gusto to convince voters of her idea. Sundew cautioned that although a poisoner couldn't climb to rob honeycomb under the eaves, the height would prevent keepers from delivering care and extra food.

A more violent swing of the ball halted the debate again. Anxious bees squirted alarm scent and guards left to investigate the disturbance. Those airborne witnessed a calamity as the swarm plummeting from the bough to splatter on the ground.

A protective cloud of bees rose above the confused mass on the ground. They grew calmer when guards returned to report no mischievous prowlers in the vicinity. They thought the branch snapped from natural causes under the weight of the swarm. The flyers landed to join others on a hypnotic march towards the source of royal perfume.

Sundew lost sight of Marigold in the chaos but felt ecstatic to be with her kin again. She listened to them nattering that a guard had seen keepers nearby. The news boded well because their guardians would never do a dastardly act to them.

Eventually, they massed in a tight space with four equal sides. The light went out as abruptly as when keepers replaced the hive cover, but their container didn't smell like home, and it bumped up and down rhythmically.

When the motion stopped, light beamed inside to lift spirits briefly before the shock of a strange, new sensation. The bees tipped on their sides slid into another heap, but the aroma of wholesome beeswax gave them immense relief. No longer panicked, they explored the comb. Although the cells contained limited honey, they wouldn't starve because an upturned bottle under the covers had holes in the lid for sucking sugar water. They stopped dreaming of new headquarters, for what could be better than to be in home sweet home?

After forced idleness from being crushed together in a swarm, the workers attended their stations early the following day. Jobs gave their lives meaning and distraction from worrying about recent events. Waxers scrambled to repair damaged cells. Gummers filled gaps between boxes and sealed mites in the Cryptum. Nurses spruced up birthing cells for the queen to lay eggs. A food production line swung into action as foragers emptied crops of nectar and unloaded pollen for restocking the pantry. Drones praised the endeavours of workers while they sipped refreshments on the side-lines.

Sundew drifted between workplaces looking for her team or a job vacancy for a waxer. Everyone seemed too busy to notice her until a dapper-looking bee pressed through the masses with a greeting.

"Golly, Marigold wasn't kidding when she said you came home. Remember our meeting in a peaceful interlude between troubles? Thanks to Sunne, we have calmer times again."

She couldn't forget Bluebell who arranged the interview with the queen. It pleased the courtier when she asked after the queen's health as a sign of loyalty.

"Daisy waited at the entrance all day until the insectors sent her away. They said you weren't coming back and had renounced your family."

So that was it! They thought she deserted them. What a fat lie! It was true she had mulled over an alternative lifestyle but only for a fleeting moment in the night far away before coming to her senses. Nowhere is better than home, the dwelling place of love, comfort, and security. Nevertheless, she wanted to know where her friends went more before catching up with home news.

"Let me make inquiries. We moved workers around and changed addresses of frames after the noirbitel rearranged the hyf. Excuse me, I have an urgent errand."

The courtier vanished into the crowd before Sundew could explain her long absence wasn't taken willingly. Alone again, she worried if her deeds would be believed without the backup of witnesses. Better to only say she lost her way home than boast of a hero's journey.

Busy workers whirling past left her once more feeling in a tizzy about what to do. She dreaded if they thought she looked as idle as a drone. Apart from herself, only a pair of bees loitered aimlessly. She sensed a flicker of furtive eyes watching her before she recognised them. And when the pair slowly approached, they halted to whisper a private conversation as if unsure of meeting her. She prepared for disappointment.

"We thought you were finished with us," Daisy said. "Did you come back to brag about your rare flower or gloat about our family disaster?"

"We saw you with a posh friend," Hyacinth added. "I suppose we aren't good enough for you now."

This wasn't the blissful reunion Sundew dreamed of. The day wouldn't end in celebration with her team, sucking nectar together and singing Auld Lang Syne. They believed the gossip. She wasn't gifted with fine words for expressing deep feelings, so she turned around to bury herself in the anonymous crowd.

Amma was right. The social lives of honeybees are complicated. If her best friends rejected her and Marigold and Bluebell disappeared abruptly without an explanation, what did others think? Perhaps she wasn't welcome anymore. She felt more at ease when she met Skunkie and Hemlock than being with her own brood.

Her life turned upside down. You don't belong in a home unless someone misses you. How could she have fooled herself for so long? Bees prefer the company of those with similar stripes whereas she was an unstriped half-queen. After travelling abroad, she knew how to survive among strangers in the wilderness. Sometimes a lonely and agonising experience, it trained her for life as a wanderer.

She flew out of the hive, but only as far as the garden to ride a bobbing head of lavender for its soothing balm. How she envied workers shuttling food to the hive, putting community ahead of their own appetites. A solo bee is impoverished from only having selfish needs and wants.

A low buzzing behind sounded like a hint not to hog the flower. On turning to apologise, Sundew was confronted with a grizzled face and two huge eyes.

"Deadnettle! What brought you out?"

"Marigold told us you came back, and I came out when we couldn't find you inside. I brought someone who's bursting to see you again."

"Shady!" Sundew recoiled, but the deputy didn't seem surprised or offended by her reaction.

"Give me a hug, comrade—"

Sundew stiffened as the bee who had led her into peril twice before rushed forward to embrace her. Deadnettle spoke for the deputy who was too overwhelmed with joy and remorse.

"She moped about losing her boss and friends and thought you died with them after scaring the monster away. I never saw her more thrilled than when she heard you are safe. Marigold said we wouldn't be back in our old home if the smaelbitel hadn't followed you back from the garden."

"You saved the hyf," the deputy blubbered.

"You must go inside to tell everyone the full story,"

Deadnettle said.

"There's no point where you aren't wanted."

He sighed, no longer the diffident drone she first knew. "Don't feel sorry for yourself. Your family is frothing with enthusiasm to greet their hero."

News that Sundew had been found flashed ahead of arrival to the hive where crowds cheered at the entrance. Workers had permission to leave their stations to stand waving in lines that wound across several combs. At the end of the parade, Bluebell waited with a group of officials to give a speech.

"Welcome home, Sunnedew. Sorry I had to hurry away to bring news to the Cwen. She proclaims this a holiday for celebrating your homecoming in our renovated home. Hardships made you stronger and the allure of foreign lands couldn't keep you from the home where you belong. We want to know about your adventures in all their tiny details for Sage to preserve in the family archives.

"Stewards uncap the nectar and let the dancing begin."

Workers and drones crowded around to congratulate Sundew on an epic journey. Bees who couldn't get close rubbed feelers with those who did, so they could feel a connection with the celebrity. However, Sundew's joy was incomplete without her best friends.

She retired from the party to a quiet corner to reflect on an extraordinary turnaround. Deadnettle came looking for her to convey a private request for a meeting.

Daisy stepped out of the shadows with feelers spread wide to declare: "Friends forever!"

Then Hyacinth followed with a greeting: "Hail, partner!"

The pair apologised for putting trust in rumours about Sundew's absence above their knowledge of her character. She felt sorry for going off in a huff without trying to explain hurt feelings. They all laughed when she asked to be forgiven for not bringing them the gift of pollen from her flower.

"There's no reunion sweeter than when old friends make friends anew," Hyacinth said.

She wondered if turning enemies into allies was even more touching than making friends again if it healed old grievances and wounds. To avoid missing the party any longer, she only had time to tell them the moving stories of Skunkie's revelation and Hemlock's last stand.

They joined the multitude toasting the queen's health. Nothing could spoil the harmony now. And if tranquillity ever became boring, they vowed never to complain.

Sundew and Daisy often flew together on sunny days. After checking for fresh blooms in the garden, they explored the countryside to sample new flavours. On finding charcoal and ashes while gathering heather pollen on the moor, they became solemn to remember relatives who perished in the Great Fire.

Sundew wanted to go further to introduce her friend to the solitary bee who offered hospitality while she was lost. But then she dismissed the idea, saying that Amma lived too far away, and the most profound respect you can pay a hermit is to leave her alone.

The leg injury kept Hyacinth inside the hive. Still, she earned a promotion for honourable service to become the senior manager of honey cooks. When the other two returned home from forays, the friends were inseparable and nicknamed the Terrific Trio. As a honey connoisseur, Deadnettle was appointed an assistant to Hyacinth as the official taster. Workers who still looked down on drones were shocked when they welcomed him to their group. But, by and by, the Trio evolved to become known as the Fabulous Four.

The hive grew strong again with help from their keepers and the fading of disruptive hostilities. The foursome rose early every morning to savour a new day and give thanks for a summer that seemed unending.

The bee family hunkered down earlier on cooler nights as autumn approached. One evening, however, felt as sweltering as in July. Daisy couldn't sleep despite being fatigued from working all day in the fields.

"I need to cool off. Does anyone want to come outside?" She expected Sundew would join her.

"Watch out for bats," Hyacinth warned.

Deadnettle tagged along as a lookout as he had the best night vision. Hyacinth hurried to catch up, peeved to be left behind,

"Gosh, it's still hot," Daisy announced at the entrance. "And there's a nasty odour in the air, though not the same as before, so let's scout around to see."

Bees rarely take night flights, as hazardous as they are futile. Predators lurk for unwary insects and some flowers close their petals to pollinators. The group kept in close formation to watch the stunning displays of moths flitting ghostly white in the moonlight, brighter than they ever saw in daytime. Hyacinth turned back to the hive, leaving them to have fun chasing mosquitoes.

She hadn't gone far before shrieking at them to return. They were bewildered by tongues of flames licking the sides of the hive from under the bottom box. As young bees, none of them had seen flames before. They would have been mesmerised if the scorching heat didn't repel them. Wisps of smoke curled out of the slit and a guard sounded the alarm:

"FIRE! FIRE! FIRE . . . !"

They knew the cautionary warning when a keeper smoked the hive, but it sounded louder and more urgently this time. The announcer's voice paused several times for a coughing fit. A roar of beating wings and stamping feet inside meant the family had woken.

Nothing strikes greater fear than a home fire. The residents knew all parts of a hive are flammable and the queen had witnessed the incineration of moorland beehives in the Great Fire. The friends watched in horror, feeling powerless to help others escape or rescue larvae roasting in the nursery. Wax fell from combs in molten blobs through the wire mesh to fuel the fire below and make billows of black smoke.

Hyacinth flew down to beg evacuees for news of the queen. They came out gulping for air and only one could speak. "I heard attendants advising her to take refuge in the top to avoid the fire," she said.

"That's barmy advice. Rising heat will trap her under

the covers unless the noirbitel comes."

Daisy agreed the only exit was via the slit after hurrying past the most intense heat underneath. "It may not be too late. A rescuer who goes inside can bring the Cwen out the same way through the smoke."

"That's suicidal! Who would dare?" Hyacinth looked horrified, but she knew who would take such a risk. Her partner meant to volunteer and was too stubborn to deter when she set her mind on a mission.

"There's no higher duty than to save a cwen."

"You won't go in alone," Sundew said to more amazement. 'There's no one with greater experience of danger."

"You will get in the way as I struggle against the stream evacuating the hyf. Wait here until you find another role."

"You called us friends forever, Daisy. We belong together either here or in a hereafter."

Daisy flashed a knowing look at Hyacinth before alighting at the entrance. She waited for a gap between bees lurching out into the volcanic night. Sundew yapped at Hyacinth for not stopping her partner. The manner of Daisy's departure was like her own disappearance in the Cryptum, a final wave to her friends too distracted by arguing to notice until she had gone.

Sundew yelled as the inferno grew fiercer, "Daisy, Daisy, I miss you already!"

The hellfire would consume the entire hive if the keepers didn't arrive soon to quench the flames. The heat bubbled paint from the walls to expose bare wood before turning it into charcoal.

Sundew hovered as close to the slit as she dared without getting singed. Before the chance to bolt inside, someone knocked her down on the grass. Supposing it was an accident in the turmoil, she turned to see who had crashed into her and saw her friend getting on her feet.

"I had to let her go and stop you," Hyacinth said. "Daisy felt compelled by a duty that even overrode our vow to care for each other. Don't throw your life away on an impulse. She believed you have another destiny. Don't call it luck to survive many trials. Even the precise timing of stepping outside before the fire could trap you is a sign of something more than chance. There's a reason for the Sunne's blessing, although too early to be seen.

"See the grief on the faces of swusters flying around, confused and leaderless. They can't rejoice at a narrow escape from death while they fear a second death even more. I mean the extinction of our family."

"There's no point in living without a cwen or friends. I

finally understood when I faced a life as a wanderer."

"Don't despair. There's hope while life hangs on, even if on a thread. We are all better off with a half-cwen than no cwen at all."

"I don't know why Daisy called me that, except to make me feel better. I never felt like a broody cwen. My life would have been easier if I looked like a normal bee and wasn't treated with scorn or used for political gain. Size and strength are the assets of a warrior bee, and that ambition conflicts with the Beeattitudes."

Deadnettle interrupted with news from scouting around the hive. "I saw a four-legs who may have set the fire. It could be the poisoner who came back angry with us for returning."

Sundew went off in a rage to fly in circles around it. She couldn't be sure if it was the same monster she tackled before because it was covered in a protective white shell. There were no visible targets on its head for her pent-up wrath. Without the pleasure of stinging it, she had to enjoy the sight of flames that had jumped from the hive on its legs.

"Don't waste your strength. Save it for others," Hyacinth pleaded. "We need a miracle to save us from a cruel world."

CHAPTER 19
A Blessed Bone

Fewer people visited the abbey or its shop after the tourist season. Joe relished a peaceful week before the new school year began. He worked in the bee-yard most mornings, trusted with routine work while the monk was laid up in the infirmary with a strained back. He inspected the grey hives every week and checked his own hive daily. It never attracted a swarm. He still regretted it didn't house the Peacemaker brood they installed in the restored painted hive.

His mother read aloud a letter enclosed with a book for Joe that Emily sent soon after returning to London. He groaned to hear her request to visit Oldburgh again during the Easter break. If she had another scheme, he hoped it would be forgotten in six months.

The blissful holidays ended on the first day of the new term at Breadcaster High School. He left home early for a seat behind the bus driver. The diesel engine rumbled into life and coughed exhaust fumes as the gang arrived just in time. He felt them glowering as they clambered on board to the back.

He felt more contented than a year earlier. He had an absorbing new pastime and the dignity of wearing long flannel trousers for the first time and a purple jacket with the school's crest. His mum treated him more like a young man around the house and he impressed Miss Higgins by arriving in class with a bulging satchel on time. Fortunately, the teacher never mentioned reports from his former school.

He celebrated the first Saturday morning by heading to the bee-yard for inspections he didn't have time for on weekdays. But the next day, he mooned around the home because the monastery forbade work on its grounds on the Sabbath. The evening arrived with the crushing anxiety of evading the gang in the morning.

His mum attended church more frequently since the funeral a year earlier. Joe grumbled at losing an hour on a free day, but she insisted he attend for his saint's day.

"Do I have to go? We went last month."

He knew she wouldn't relent when she dressed in her best jacket and hat. After buttoning his collar, she sent him upstairs for a tie.

"Vespers is short. You can bring your new book if you read it discreetly before the service."

The book had a Goliath beetle on the glossy cover under

its title: *The World of Big and Belligerent Bugs*. The sender wrote inside: *Give my love to the stingers. Emmy X.*

Strolling to the abbey, mother and son felt the first nip of autumnal air. By the time they entered the nave, the sky had turned from orange to blood red as the sun dipped below dark clouds. A small congregation waited in silence, absorbing the fragrance of smouldering frankincense. Joe sidled along an empty pew, leaving the cushion for his mum to sit behind an old lady in a bonnet.

The side door creaked open on the first strike of the hour in the clock tower. A tap on the shoulder told him to close the book as the congregation stood. His mum knew the proper responses—when to stand, sit, kneel and cross herself. Monks trooped in with bowed heads and hands buried in opposite baggy sleeves. After assembling in front to pray, they chanted a psalm.

Meanwhile, Joe's butterfly mind flitted around the building. He counted lights on a candlestand, ogled at images in windows, and wondered who carved their initials on the back of the pew. Reopening the book to a chapter about tropical insects, he became so immersed he didn't notice his bum going numb on the wooden seat.

The old lady twisted around at the sound of pages turning and smiled at his mother, supposing her pious son studied the missal. Joe paused at a sentence that put a former terror into perspective: *The sting of a bullet ant feels like walking on red hot coals, the most painful sting in the world.*

Despite the absorption in reading and detachment from the ritual, he had remarkably alert ears. He was first to jump to his feet at the final amen before the monks filed out.

While his mum nattered to the lady in the courtyard, Joe searched for Cuthbert. Hard to see in the gloaming, he eventually found the black-robed monk huddled in conversation with a villager. They discussed the faint glow over the orchard. The gardener would have known if he left a bonfire unattended, and it was too early for Guy Fawkes celebrations, not that they were allowed on Catholic property anyway.

"I wonder what it means. The sun never sets that far west even in midsummer," Cuthbert said.

"Eery to see it over the graveyard," the other man said.

The boy slunk back to his mum to drop the book in her bag before leaving at a trot. He headed off to check the shed full of woodenware and flammable liquids, although without electricity to make a spark it wasn't at risk unless someone deliberately set it on fire.

He breathed a sigh of relief at the gate since the shed was absorbed into the blackness. Only a rosy tint on a creosoted siding drew him to look on the other side.

Even the scene of a ruined hive several weeks earlier didn't leave him as gobsmacked as to see it ablaze that evening. Flames curled around boxes from a source underneath and sparks ascended in the smoke. Of all the hazards to bees, he never imagined a hive could catch fire. He should have known better because only minutes ago, he had seen beeswax candles burning merrily in the abbey.

The second shock was to see a figure dressed from head to foot in white dancing and cursing nearby. The outfit looked too similar to Emily's bee suit to be mistaken for the grave clothes of a phantom.

Joe fumed at the demon he presumed responsible for the fire. After caring for the hive and recovering the swarm, he took the attack personally. A few weeks before, he had no sympathy for stinging insects and smirked at the monk for treating them like friends. No longer. He even felt remorse from accidentally squashing a bee when replacing hive covers. The chasm he formerly perceived between humans and insects had drawn close from observing their joy and struggle for life.

If only the monk had listened to him, the raider might not have come back for this diabolical evil. Emily said criminals always return to the scene of their crime in detective novels. After bungling his first attempt to steal the box by poisoning, Brad tried to drive the bees out with smoke. He was foiled again from not realising that beeswax is highly combustible and by letting the fire get out of control. Standing too close, his leggings had caught alight around the ankles.

Joe gloated at the tortured face blinded by smoke he imagined behind the mask. The boy was the meanest kid in school and never the brightest tack. Yet, it felt shameful to gape like a spectator at a heretic burning at the stake.

He snapped to attention on hearing voices along the path. What would they say if they knew he casually watched someone suffer? But what could he do without a watering hose or fire extinguisher? The villain didn't realise that frantic movements fanned the flames and patting with gloves spread them to other places. The wax sheen on the suit taken from the shed was a fire hazard that Joe had made doubly incendiary by soaking in turpentine a few days earlier.

The figure fumbled with clumsy gloves for the zip fastener to get out of the suit before getting scorched. He ought to roly-poly in the dewy grass to extinguish the flames. When urgent advice went unheeded, Joe snuck up behind to trip him over. The body sprawled on the ground and lay still.

Joe didn't want to be found with the culprit. As torchlights flashed closer between trees, he dropped to his knees to nudge the arms against the side of the body. They didn't resist, perhaps grateful to be helped.

"Roll over!" he roared, pushing the heavy body through two complete rotations to quench the flames. He leapt back to avoid the gloves flung off. Then a hand could pull the zip from chin to crotch for wriggling out of sleeves and leggings. When the hooded veil finally lifted, it didn't expose a pink face in the firelight but a full beard.

"Mr. Grattich!"

So Brad's old man was the raider and had probably goaded his son into bullying Joe for the deed. He didn't care about the welfare of bees when he drove them out with mothballs, or minded how many died in the fire. Impelled by an old grudge and greedy for treasure, he got nothing for his acts and destroyed what he craved.

The man stopped cursing when he recognised Joe after stumbling to his feet. He cocked his head to hear voices and a click of the gate latch. Then, after gently ruffling Joe's mop of hair, he fled into the night.

Joe lay in the grass, gazing at the stars and smelling turps from touching the suit. He heard a hissing extinguisher and men calling for pails of water. As he stealthily dragged the suit to the shed, the people appeared in silhouette against the orange firelight. He hoped to slip away but hadn't noticed someone approaching, swathed in black.

"Is that you, Joe?" Cuthbert called out of the darkness. "Did you see anyone?"

"Nah. This the last straw for prize bees."

Cuthbert made an audible sigh. "Your mother wants you to go straight home for tomorrow is a school day."

He left the men damping flames and took the boundary path for its solitude to help him think.

Would anything valuable remain in the cold ashes of day? Would his mum force him to declare what he knew? Of the three wise monkeys in her china set on the Welsh dresser, one covered its mouth: *Speak no evil.* No good could come out of exposing Mr. Grattich as the arsonist any more than from accusing his son of kidnapping. He wouldn't drive a deeper wedge between their families. As for the monk, he had to stew over an unsolved mystery.

The following morning, a friend sitting next on the bus asked if he heard about a fire on the monastery grounds. To avoid a definite reply, Joe gave a muffled grunt. Then a hand on his shoulder made him cringe as the gang boarded.

Brad leaned over so close that Joe could smell fried bacon on his breath.

After the bus pulled away, he swivelled for a discreet glance to the back. Brad smiled and gave a thumbs-up. The grunts beside him lifted their thumbs, too, as they always followed the leader. The only explanation for the friendly gestures Joe could think of was if Brad was told to make peace by his father.

The journey continued uneventfully until the kids were dropped off at school. Joe no longer needed to take refuge in the classroom during the break to avoid an ambush in the playground. Miss Higgins had misread his presence for diligence and so she was disappointed when he didn't stay after lessons anymore. She snapped at him in the last lesson for gazing out the window.

After changing clothes at home, Joe rushed past his mum before she could order him to avoid the monastery. The monk had left the infirmary against doctor's orders.

He almost bumped into a woman taking a bundle of second-hand clothes into the Oxfam shop. Brad and Pete lounged against the butcher's shop wall with cigarettes dangling from their lower lips, still in school uniform. They nodded as he hot-footed past.

He took a wide circle to avoid the shed after seeing the monk lolling in his deckchair outside. The sun shone, birds twittered, and the meadow appeared as verdant as ever. Everything seemed normal, as if no calamity had happened the night before. Then he saw the hive. A blackened hull of sodden charcoal had collapsed to half its former height. He squatted to poke the ring of ash with a stick until his hamstrings ached, but stood on hearing a rustling robe behind.

"Who can hate these innocents that much? A part of me is missing."

Joe knew how it felt to grieve. A regimental officer brought news from the war front to their doorstep the previous year. He had dashed upstairs to throw himself on the bed and heard his mother sobbing in the next room afterwards. They mourned in private, sharing more in their eyes than in words, and didn't need advice from well-meaning outsiders. Instead of showing pity on his face, he hoped the monk saw a shared grief.

"I'm too old to start again, Joe," the monk said as he sauntered back to flop in the chair.

If a glasshouse stood nearby, the boy might have smashed it with stones to purge his rage. The monk's project seemed ill-fated no matter how many times they rebuilt the hive. The savagery of the attack broke a golden thread tying the monk to a noble mission. He had other hives but only Peacemakers in his heart. Other keepers would breed prize bees in future, but the monk's legacy would be erased as new grass grows over burnt earth. The man wrapped in a robe didn't have time on his side; he looked like a bundle of old clothes for recycling at Oxfam.

Perhaps something could be salvaged from the ruin, even if the monk couldn't bear to look. Joe separated the burnt shells of boxes, careless of blackening his hands. The frames stuck with propolis and toasted wax needed force to be separated. Those not wholly destroyed dripped honey from broken cells into pools with floating bees.

He found a fuzzy ball of insects between two adjacent frames. They clustered like that in winter to protect the queen, and perhaps the workers tried to insulate her from the furnace heat. Peeling off corpses, he found a golden insect with singed wings and a dot of yellow pigment on its back. He buried it under a stone so the monk wouldn't find it.

The bottom box had suffered the most damage as closest to the fire. After removing frames turned into brittle charcoal, Joe found a smaller box resting on the wire mesh. A layer of propolis prevented it from burning, like an asbestos coat. His mind started to wheel again. Was this the box his grandad presented to Abbot Wilfrid when they built the new abbey, the same as medieval monks hid from the royal commissioners? The Grattiches would glare if they could see him now; Emily would cry with delight.

The monk ignored the racket he made from ripping off the wooden sides to extract the box. The thrill of discovery faded on finding it too light to be a treasure trove and only the size of a shoebox. Joe hoped the monk wouldn't gripe if he peeped inside. It took a great deal of scraping with his knife to remove the crust of propolis for its original form and beauty to emerge.

Crafted by ancient monks or lay brothers to resemble a church, the box had a veneer of blue enamel with a copper overlay to portray monks or friars on a pilgrimage. Joe carried it to the monk, expecting to cheer him up and take his mind off bees for a while.

The monk didn't even bat an eyelid. He had guarded it for umpteen years in a painted hive among the grey ones before moving it near the shed when the Peacemaker queen arrived. If his abbot had instructed him to keep the box in the hive, he would have obeyed without asking questions. Monks are not supposed to care about personal possessions, but he ought to be glad to know it was safe.

The monk's manner seemed to give permission to open the box. Joe bent his blade from attempting to lever the roof off, so he brought a mallet and chisel from the shed. A museum curator would have a heart attack to see him whacking the box because it alone was a treasure.

Although his expectations had plunged, a few ancient coins or pieces of jewellery would do fine. But even that timid hope was crushed when the roof finally came off. The monk leaned forward, looking as surprised as Joe felt disappointed to see only yellow sand. From the monk's expression, it seemed the abbot never let on about the secret, and perhaps even he didn't know the trouble over it was for nothing. And yet almost beyond doubt, the box had once held valuables owned by an ancient monastery before a treasure hunter found it.

Dipped in the sand, Joe's fingers found a few desiccated bees. Groping inside again, he pulled out a grey knobbly object, like the hollow stub of a tree branch. Did the thief leave it as a hoax for the next person to find, maybe hundreds of years later? He prepared to sling it over his shoulder when a shout startled him, and he looked into the monk's wild eyes.

"Stop! Give me Saint Eadwig's bone."

He handed the object to trembling hands for the monk to bless and kiss. Mrs. Brawson would be appalled, saying it was unhygienic and could contain plague germs, but her son stayed quiet, dumbfounded by the change of manner.

"Abbot Wilfrid promised the box would bless our bees," the monk said, coming out of a trance to his senses. "He assured me it didn't contain anything of worldly value because nothing unholy has that power. It all makes sense now. Pilgrims came to venerate the relics of saints and they hallowed Eadwig for defending the first beehives. The Oldburgh brood has flourished for years under his guardianship, although he hasn't managed to defend the Peacemakers from a curse on them."

So what if the secret was an old bone? Joe still didn't get why it aroused so much feeling. He felt cheated as if he found a stone inside a gift-wrapped Christmas present. How could anyone believe in the power of a long-dead hermit? The recent spate of crimes against the hive proved the folly of magical thinking. The village would never have suffered from convulsions of greed if the box had never been discovered in the first place or if the abbot reburied it in the graveyard.

He left the monk see-sawing between grief for losing bees and euphoria at finding a relic. A drizzle of rain made his shirt feel as damp as his spirits. If Eadwig's bone had supernatural powers, it would have commanded the heavens to rain hard enough to dowse the fire. But instead, it was responsible for evil that annihilated prize bees and spoiled his new love.

He had looked forward to a colony of his own in the starter hive where he would be like a forester transplanting saplings to a plantation. A storm blew down hope. He stalked off, determined to leave beekeeping behind. Butterfly collecting was never so discouraging.

The sight of the little hive made him irritated. It never attracted a swarm and would fester without bees to occupy it. The care he gave to making boxes and frames was a waste of time for things fit for firewood. He kicked it, but only made it shudder instead of falling off the blocks.

A bee flew out of the slit, a second bee appeared, and then another went inside. *That's funny!* Bees are inquisitive creatures constantly on the lookout for food, so why would they visit empty boxes?

Joe removed the covers to inspect the boxes. A few bees waddled along the edge of frames. He started to hum as he lifted the first frame. The comb was covered in a mat of bees busily drawing wax to make new cells. He found the same in the next frame and the next.

Was this the feral swarm he dreamt of attracting? It could be an offshoot from the grey hives if a young queen left with some workers to avoid confronting the reigning monarch. He would enjoy stumping the monk who said swarms don't happen that late in the season, but what if the man was right? Where, then, did the bees come from? He trembled to think if survivors of the prized colony took up residence, just as he always wanted. The colour of their stripes would tell—tan for grey hive residents or brown for the Peacemaker brood . . .

CHAPTER 20

Aftermath

While the fire still raged, the last residents to emerge safely from the hive joined a boiling cloud of bees nearby. Without the aroma of honeycomb, they didn't know where to fly; without the queen's perfume, they didn't know who to follow. The three survivors of the Fabulous Four searched the cloud for friends and teammates who survived the inferno. They rendezvoused near the hedge to exchange news in the firelight.

"Why did our swusters trail after you, Sunnedew?" Hyacinth asked.

"Look, they keep coming," said Deadnettle.

They suspended their conversation to watch the trickle following Sundew grow into a cone of ever-larger numbers. Eventually, the entire cloud transported to surround them.

"What do they want?" Sundew asked, feeling the gaze of thousands of eyes.

"They want a leader, Dewy. Do you know a haven where we can be safe?" Hyacinth asked.

Sundew led the swarm to the empty hive on the other

side of the shed. The junior keeper had furnished it with wax foundation boards in lustrous frames. It was large enough to accommodate the reduced size of the Peacemaker family.

The next day they began to make it habitable and smell homely. Comb-maidens built rows of cells for a nursery and the pantry. Field bees flitted to the garden to gather food. They worked urgently with autumn coming, but one rainy afternoon, senior hive officials announced a suspension of work so they could attend a general assembly.

A new storyteller took the stage in the top box. She drew murmurs from an audience who wondered if Forget-Me-Not could match the renowned speeches of her predecessor.

"Dear swusters and broders," she began. "We have endured troubles and threats in these momentous times and lost our beloved Cwen Goldenrod, the eminent Sage, and many brave defenders of the hyf. But besides mourning for them, we are thankful to be at peace again and to Sunne for rising faithfully every morning.

"Let us celebrate our connection to all living families. It's easy to be neighbourly to our close kin in the lower meadow, but we are also cousins of four-legs and feather-wings, flies and worms, and have even more remote relatives. Imagine the world as one vast hyf we share with every creature and plant. If we believe we are connected to them, we ought to mourn their losses, pity their wounds, feel hunger when they starve, share their joys, and honour their stories. But, of course, it's hard to think of so many, and very demanding to sympathise with our enemies.

"Don't be fooled into thinking a fulfilled life can be independent of others, even those you don't like. We are like leaves, roots, and blossoms joined to the same trunk. We grow and fall to spin the cycle of life. So I urge you not to grieve for your dear hive mates forever. Although departed, they haven't completely 'gone'. They have left echoes of their presence in our homes and bodies, and dearest of all, in our memories. There is no final and absolute death until the humming world stops.

"Think what it means to be a bee. We weren't brought into the world for our own pleasure but for pollinating plants, so all our cousins can have flourishing lives. This role for keeping earth families healthy requires love, duty, and courage, the virtues that Cwen Goldenrod championed and Sage called the Beeattitudes.

"Never surrender to despair if the great cycle will stop. We have lost our modor but Sunne has brought us another. A new fragrance in the hyf unites us for a new era. I saw the new cwen flying with Broder Deadnettle before she opened a new comb in the nursery today. Give thanks to Sunne for new birth.

"Finally, it gives me great pleasure to announce a royal appointment. Please give a warm welcome to the Speaker of the Congregation who will deliver her first broadcast."

Hyacinth came out of the crowd to cheers, dragging a hind leg.

"History never did run as straight as a beeline," she began. "We are unprepared for outrageous misfortunes that tumble out of the blue, stealing control of our lives and injuring innocent society.

"And yet, we are resilient insects down the ages by preserving a strong and generous community that supports innumerable cousins who depend on the fertility of plants we guarantee through pollination. But a society governed by rigid laws and customs is forever hive-bound, too slow to react or adapt to new opportunities or circumstances forced on us. We would still be nesting in hollow trees, rejecting four-legged friends and scared of monsters except for the courage and inspiration of individuals.

"We owe our deliverance from peril to two family members. My partner Daisy was an ordinary comb-maiden, like you and me. She could pass unnoticed in a crowd yet represented the best of us. She made choices that others ridiculed, and decisions costly to herself. We thrive again because she had faith in a newbie who wanted to belong yet had to contend with hostility, temptations, and numerous dangers for being different.

"That bee now reigns as the peacemaker, Cwen Sunnedew. Her life hasn't flown straight. Before she knew what she could be, she was a weaxer, prisoner, battle commander, and a traveller. She even fancied becoming a storyteller. Instead, she has become *our story* and the first among equals at the end of history."

* * * * * * * *

Emily came down to Oldburgh midweek before Easter. She hoped the country air would inspire her to write and looked forward to a sandwich lunch with Brother Cuthbert on the garden bench for old times' sake. Privately, she wanted to check the hive with the monk's special brood.

After breakfast on the first morning, her aunt asked if she had finished the story about black magic honey

"Oh, that," she replied, ignoring Joe's smug face. "I decided to write about last summer's events in the bee-yard instead. I call it *The Oldburgh Treasure*. A family friend in the book trade might publish it if I check the facts and get permission from people. Mum and Dad are excited to have a debut author and plan for a book signing event."

"That's wonderful news and clever to have a title with a double meaning. I hope it helps Brother Adam recover after the horrid publicity about that silly box."

"It's mostly about his bees. I'm going with Joe the next time he makes an inspection."

"Be careful because Brother Adam hasn't replaced your suit he threw away," her aunt said. "Joe doesn't wear his outfit, which looks as fresh as the day I made it."

Joe rolled his eyes. "Aw, Mum, they are gentle bees."

"Hasn't he been stung yet, Auntie? He will need to be more careful when his voice breaks as a teenager if they don't recognise a lower hum."

Won't she ever stop teasing? Joe huffed.

"Gosh, I'm keeping my customers waiting at the door." Mrs. Brawson rushed out of the room, flustered by the chiming clock and left them alone.

"I saw the abbey service on telly when the abbot buried the bone," Emily said. "It looked like the entire village turned out for the ceremony. Is the whole story out, or are you holding something back?"

Joe narrowed his eyes. "After a lot of nonsense, the gossip fizzled out because the abbot didn't want a police investigation and decided the relic was a matter for church authorities. Mum and Cuthbert were curious if I saw the fire-raiser, but no one else knows I was there first. The old monk thinks my hive saved his bees by some miracle. Without a lucky bone inside to protect them, he calls me their guardian angel." He chuckled.

"The villain who set a fire to steal treasure didn't even get an old bone," she snickered. "You never told me who, but I guess it was that mug or Brad's father. The Grattiches choked on their greed."

"Don't juice up the story by including the gamekeeper's family. They will deny having anything to do with the monastery. When mum saw old Grattich in line at the post office, he blustered when asked about his bandaged hands."

Emily giggled. "The local wildlife is safer since he can't pull a trigger."

She assured him that nothing she wrote would embarrass his family or the monastery. There were two stories told in parallel that overlapped, especially at the climax when all seemed lost. Nevertheless, it ended happily for the beekeeper and closed a village mystery.

"I knew you wouldn't mention visiting the tomb," Joe said, "and I'm relieved you left out the poison and arson attacks. It's a wishy-washy story, though, that doesn't explain the fire."

"I puzzled over that for a long time until Dad showed me a newspaper. It quoted an old villager who thought the hive was struck by lightning, so I left it at that because few readers will remember it was a clear day. If I were writing fiction, I would blame Abbot Godwin for praying to heaven for a bolt to hit the hive." Joe burst into laughter.

She asked how Brother Adam coped with a grilling from the abbot for concealing a holy relic and with reporters dropping into the yard without warning for interviews. The stress had sent the monk back to bed in the infirmary. Emily hoped a story of his devotion to bees would warm the hearts of readers and prevent the abbot from closing the bee-yard.

She called the new queen Peacemaker II to please the monk. But he doubted that the queen in the little hive could be a refugee from the peacemaker brood, and Joe couldn't be sure. She came back to Oldburgh to find out because that loose end had to be tied before a final draft of her book.

"I desperately hope the hive doesn't contain only some lingering workers of the prize brood without a queen. My book contract will then be in jeopardy. The publisher says it makes a much stronger story to have a continuous thread."

"I haven't checked to avoid chilling frames that might contain eggs and baby bees. We can inspect the hive on Good Friday when it's forecasted as the first warm day."

Two days later, they visited the orchard where Joe had

transferred the hive to shelter under an apple tree in winter. Emily grinned at the artwork on the sides: a painting of white crossbones. The colony appeared vigorous, judging by traffic at the entrance and contented buzzing in the canopy above, speckled with pink and white blossoms.

Joe searched the nursery frames as the most likely places to find a queen. But without a yellow mark on her back, it was harder to identify her from the myriad of workers. Eventually, he found her squatting over a cell to lay an egg and nudged her attendants aside for a better view.

"There she is," he shrieked and pointed a finger. "Whoopee! She's got the same scar as the queen we saw before."

"Careful you don't hurt her, Joe."

Holding up the frame for closer examination, the cousins recalled previous encounters with the insect. Joe expected her to cry at the sight, but her eyes stayed dry with a glazed, far-off look. She was working through the arc of her story to close the book. The bee they found and lost and found again came home.

"The monk will go wild when he hears, and so will your publisher," he said. "But don't think it's the whole story without the bees' history. You don't know their language, and they wouldn't tell anyway."

They left the solitary hive for the meadow to take a short tour around the other hives. Emily nodded approval of how Joe had cared for them, leaving candy inside before the spring nectar flow. Since all hives were active, he projected an excellent harvest that year. But he wouldn't collect honey from the peacemaker brood because precious bees needed extra food to raise royal daughters for fulfilling the monk's dream.

Joe wasn't a natural chatterbox, but he didn't stop yammering that morning. Emily paid him polite attention, but her mind was still mostly elsewhere. He didn't take offence as they respected the other's passion: she liked bees but loved books and the other way around for him.

"I had a postcard from America with a picture of honeybees," he said, still straining to get attention.

"Oh, I didn't know you made a pen-pal over there," she said.

"He's a beekeeper I met in the shop last summer and signed the card, Chuck Stinger."

"That's a funny name. So what else did he write?"

I thought you would like to bee.

Saying Thanks

I grew up in London and became a scientist and author in England, Scotland and Canada before settling in the USA. When I finally had time to be an amateur naturalist and beekeeper, I wrote this debut in children's literature under a pen name.

My beekeeping began when the corner of a churchyard was set aside as a bee-yard (apiary) by the rector, Carleton Bakkum, and the late Nannie Milliner. I learned the craft by trial and error with help from the Colonial Beekeepers Association and my Uncle John, who kept bees in England for forty years. But I owe most of my education to generations of bees in my hives; they inspired this story and nourished my family and neighbours. I forgive them for every sting, for who am I to grumble when I took their honey?

Two artists have graced this book with their work. Illustrations by the Cornish artist Kim Lynch capture settings I imagined, and Elizabeth Ogle from Maine painted the gorgeous cover.

This story combines a fantasy about the lives of bees

with the real world of people who care for them. I tried to be as faithful as possible in fiction to insect biology and beekeeping lore as an educator and researcher. This required more creative writing than in my scientific mode, including British parlance and slang. Two professional editors guided this journey: Jenny Bowman in North Carolina and Amber Hatch in Oxford, England. I followed the *Economist* magazine's style of spelling and punctuation to overlap British and American conventions.

My first reader was Julie Chen, a middle-grade student in Palo Alto, California. Three schoolteachers kindly read early drafts of the manuscript: Courtney Curran and Lucy Godwin in the USA and Amanda Snaith in the UK. As I approached a publishing deadline, the distinguished Indiana author James Alexander Thom kindly offered an endorsement and advice I cherish for future projects.

The most heartfelt thanks are saved to the end for those closest to me. Lucinda was my first and final reviewer. She gave unstinting support as a gentle critic and patient spouse. Nor will I ever forget that the seeds of this book sprouted while following the wagging tails of Lilah and Ben on our favourite trails.

Rowan Gordon
June 2022

Contact the author: RowanGordonWrites@gmail.com

Postscript

Profit from sales of this book is pledged to Children with Cancer UK and the American Childhood Cancer Organization. They support causes close to my heart and career.

Printed in Great Britain
by Amazon